Emily

LACEY O'DUNN
THE ROOKIE

*Good Reading
Patricia Crandall*

Also by Patricia Crandall

Melrose, Then and Now
I Passed This Way
The Dog Men
Tales of an Upstate New York Bottle Miner
Pat's Collectibles (a collection of short stories)
Living to One Hundred Plus
The Red Gondola and the Cova
A Reunion of Death

LACEY O'DUNN
THE ROOKIE

Crime/thriller novel by
Patricia Crandall

Lacey O'Dunn, The Rookie is a work of fiction.
Names, characters, places and incidents are the products of the author's imagination or are used fictitiously. Any resemblance to actual events, locales, or persons, living or dead, is entirely coincidental.

Copyright © 2022 by Patricia Crandall
All rights reserved. No part of this book may be used or reproduced in any form, electronic or mechanical, including photocopying, recording, or scanning into any information storage and retrieval system, without written permission from the author except in the case of brief quotation embodied in critical articles and reviews.

Book design by The Troy Book Makers

Printed in the United States of America
The Troy Book Makers • Troy, New York • thetroybookmakers.com

To order additional copies of this title, contact your favorite local bookstore or visit www.shoptbmbooks.com

ISBN: 978-1-61468-752-8

CONTENTS

Chapter 1 — **The Rookie – A New Life** 1

Chapter 2 — **The Lead** 5

Chapter 3 — **Vinnie Santora** 11

Chapter 4 — **Exposed** 19

Chapter 5 — **Unlike Connections** 25

Chapter 6 — **Disclosure** 31

Chapter 7 — **The Offenders** 39

Chapter 8 — **On the Road Again** 43

Chapter 9 — **Out of Action** 51

Chapter 10 — **Mutiny** 57

Chapter 11 — **Revelation** 63

Chapter 12 — **Showdown** 67

Chapter 13 — **Missing** 75

Chapter 14 — **Venomous** 81

Chapter 15 — **Under Arrest** 93

Chapter 16 — **Together we are Strong** 99

DEDICATION

Lacey O'Dunn, The Rookie is dedicated to my children, Bonnie St. Onge and A.J. Crandall, grandchildren, Nicole, Ashley and Jeremy St. Onge - my beacons of light.

Thanks to Jennifer Murgia, Freelance Editor, www.jennifermurgia.com, who provided quality edits to make *Lacey O'Dunn, The Rookie* an exceptional read.

They have corrupted themselves; their spot is not the spot of His children; they are a perverse and crooked generation.

Deuteronomy: The Song of Moses, Verse 5

CHAPTER 1

THE ROOKIE * A NEW LIFE

Lacey O'Dunn eased her Subaru into an empty space in the Zone 5 Police Academy parking lot. She noted the time: 8:45. Perfect, considering the slick driving conditions and poor visibility caused by thick, swirling snow and ice-covered roads. Early for her appointment with Chief Tadhg Ringwood in his Central Police office at 9:10, she kept the engine running for heat and sipped coffee from the Styrofoam McDonald's cup, tasting the hot plastic with each sip. A satisfied feeling washed through her at having made it to this official moment.

She was pleased with the long-sleeved blue blouse and gray twill slacks she chose to wear for this meeting. It was understated for the training she would be subjected to in order to become a policewoman. The fur lined black leather jacket would keep her warm during winter and not draw attention to her perfect size 8 figure. It was well worth the splurge to look the part for her new profession.

A few years ago, meeting with an officer would not have been the momentous occasion that today was affording her. This was a planned meeting based on her merit, and she had every intention of soaking up its significance on the road to her career path which marked the end of a dark period in her life.

Her thoughts returned to Monday morning's recruiting ceremony and Chief Ringwood's welcome speech: "New officers are our lifeblood," the chief officer boomed in his robust voice with a distinct Irish accent. "They are the focus of an agency that keeps the importance of law and order moving for the future. New officers keep us on the cutting edge and help fuel our mission of advancing into a future of blue family members that will always protect you. On Wednesday, one young woman and six young men will begin extensive physical and psychological training at the Police Academy."

With that statement, he looked directly at each candidate, peering into their potential and untapped ability. Then he continued, "It will be a challenge, as well as time consuming. I have met with these individuals, and I feel each one is up to the task. The result will be that the streets in Troy, New York are safer for our citizens because crimes, often very serious crimes, will be solved and not shelved as cold cases. New officers extend the hand that the police station serves with, as we go from understaffed to adding officers that have the heart and tenacity to serve their community with grace and passion for justice and righteousness for the citizens that we have all sworn to protect and serve."

As he spoke, Lacey had dropped her hands to the folds of her modest blue uniform and considered the audience. Her mother, father, and grandmother, Nadia Likoudis, were seated in the middle of the first row. Her mother looked distracted, most likely fretting about not being able to light up a cigarette. Her father's blank gaze said nobody was home upstairs, meaning he had checked out to think over the next day's business dealings. Her grandmother, though, beamed at her, clearly proud of her granddaughter and elated that she had been invited to the event.

Lacey's eyes traveled to the dark paneled wall at the back of the deteriorating City Hall building. Slouched against it, with his hands shoved deep into his pockets, was Vinnie Santora. Standing next to him, dressed in too-tight skirt and leggings tucked into knee-high boots and a fleece crop top, looking battered and fragile, was his latest squeeze, Starr Ellis.

Lacey's heart skipped a beat. Why were two of the most adverse people she knew attending the police academy swearing-in ceremony? She drew a long breath, trying to control the memories that flew through her mind, past the recovery philosophies that usually stood as a boundary between the feelings and urges of the past and her future.

Vinnie's insolent eyes sized her up, as if she were still his prey. Joey McGrath, a friend, and a police academy recruit standing beside her, nudged her elbow, as if to say, 'don't pay any attention to him.' Lacey clenched her hands at her sides.

At age sixteen, Lacey had a drinking and drug problem. The wrong crowd had proven the Bible verse, 'Bad company corrupts good morals' (I Corinthians 15:33). It was completely true. She had been raised in a church-going home. Her parents had provided structure and boundaries, yet the wrong crowd had led her into the wolf's lair of partying and bad decisions. The dealers and snakes from the street world were never happy to see a customer on the road to healing and recovery, so she had been kept drunk and high until that was her norm.

With family, friends from church, and medical intervention, Lacey was able to get clean. She never wanted to repeat the day she found herself strapped to a bed in a medical facility shaking and sweating from withdrawal. It took months of rigid indoctrination and medical techniques before she felt whole. Now, at age 28, she was sober and free of drugs. She looked forward to a long career in the police force, retiring as a Master Detective and a member of the Vidocq Society.

The Vidocq Society was a Nonprofit corporation, which, by the terms of its charter, was a fraternal organization comprised of professionals and non-professionals who met in a social setting to discuss unsolved crimes. Her goals could fast track her career, with leadership behind her, as more dedicated professionals were needed to sort through the ever-growing cold case files.

Lacey pulled her eyes away from the familiar past evil staring back at her and braced herself for the fight that was to come. She wasn't sure why Vinnie was at the ceremony, but she was sure he was still involved with the criminal element she had left behind. Meaning he might become a part of her life again, albeit on the other side of the handcuffs she would soon carry.

CHAPTER 2

THE LEAD

May you be blessed by your dreams and the courage to chase them.

Diane M. Geiser Toasts:
June Cotner and Nancy Tupper Ling

At 9:00 Lacey walked into the police station, finger-combing her hair, making last minute adjustments to the stray placement by way of releasing the nervous energy using her fingertips. She leaned over to brush snow off her jacket and was nearly trampled by a tattooed youth exiting the building. Lacey caught her balance while her heart raced with the near miss. It would have been humiliating to wipe out right before her meeting with Chief Ringwood.

"You're at risk when you come into this place." Molly Baines, a legendary, middle aged desk sergeant, stocky but toned, removed her eyeglasses, and frowned. "Lacey, you have four annoying qualities."

"How do I possibly offend you?" Lacey asked, alarmed.

Molly ticked off four fingers. "You're slender, blonde, beautiful, and too smart for your own good. Why aren't you training to be a model? Instead, you're settling in for a career in this dingy place."

Lacey relaxed her stance. "I want to be in law enforcement. Are there restrictions against female cops being strong and good-looking?"

Molly gave a deep throated chuckle. "Congratulations, Ms. O'Dunn-Marple. I wish I could have been at the ceremony to give you support but someone had to take incoming calls and welcome the overnight guests."

"Thanks, Molly. I'll be put to the test with the training."

Molly wagged a finger. "Don't let the guys pass you by. A couple of formidable women are needed to stabilize this force." She drew a breath. "Heed my words. Watch your back at all times."

Lacey tapped the desk. "Molly dear, that's my motto for life. And you're right; I need to watch my back, but it's not with the guys in my unit." She stared past Molly through the smudged double-window at the thick snowflakes obliterating the view. Vinnie Santora came to mind.

"The Chief wants to see me?" Lacey asked, switching gears to tackle the reason she was here.

Molly held up a one-second finger to Lacey. "Chief's beside himself with a hodgepodge of crime sprees. He wants to nail these criminals before the press makes an abysmal show of the force." She paused. "I'll do anything to stop the reporters from harassing Chief and this division."

Lacey raised her eyebrows. "Chief Ringwood's exemplary. He's the reason I joined the force." *What could be happening that puts the entire force in the limelight, and how can I help?* Lacey's mind kicked into high gear, like it always did when there was a problem that needed to be solved.

"He needs all the help we can give him." Molly inclined her head. "Go, or he'll be in a tirade if you're late."

Lacey hurried a short distance down a narrow hall emitting the funky smell of sanitized floors and musty ground level aroma that chemicals couldn't touch. She entered a vacant cubicle where the only bright item was a Marilyn Monroe pin-up calendar hanging crooked on the wall. Without looking, Lacey was sure the calendar was years off from today's date, but that Marilyn's countenance had saved the relic from being thrown into File 13.

She pushed open a heavy wooden door and entered a large, airless office where a super odor-killer air freshener sat on a wide, expanded mahogany desk. Chief Tadhg Ringwood tilted back in his chair and crossed his wrestler's arms.

He was a young fifty of Irish Indian heritage. At birth his mother christened him with the Irish moniker, Tadhg Patrick Ringwood, after his father and paternal grandfather. He insisted on being called Tad in his civilian life and had been married and divorced three times due to his priorities—a Chief Officer first, a cop second, an investigator third, and a husband last. There had been no children. The intensity in Chief's green eyes made Lacey glad she wasn't on the interrogation side of the table but had been invited for this meeting.

Lacey sat down and shifted the chair until it stabilized.

"I'm getting straight to the point," Chief said. "Why was Vinnie Santora at the swearing-in ceremony the other day?"

Lacey opened her mouth to protest, and then thought better of it. She said, "You'll have to ask Mr. Santora."

Chief pulled a thin folder out of a pile on his desk and tapped it. "I know about your prior connection with him."

Lacey stared daggers at him, "That's history and not relevant to my present situation. I want to be treated equal, Chief, not patronized."

Chief flattened both hands on the desk and pushed back. "My concern is this city's burgeoning with crime and Santora's name crosses my desk as a viable offender with every official charge. Yet, in each case, someone takes the rap for him, leaving him clean." He snapped a pencil in half. "I'm challenging my team to help me nail this guy. I'm turning over every leaf, and if you can give me information concerning his activities, I'd appreciate it."

In her chalk-white face, Lacey's eyes widened. "Chief Ringwood, I wish I'd never met Vinnie Santora. Thank God I'm where I'm at now. I had a great deal of help getting to this point thanks to my family and friends, like Joey McGrath, who never gave up on me." She lowered her eyes to the cluttered desk, attempting to focus on a staple remover, and continued in a feverish rush. "No thanks to the crisis centers, counseling services the county provides, 911, or state troopers and local sheriffs. Those departments are not equipped to help family members aid addicts hooked on drugs or alcohol to live a functional life."

Chief narrowed his eyes. "Let's leave this lecture about dysfunctional county and government services for another time, shall we, Miss O'Dunn?" He looked unyielding as he asked, "You mentioned McGrath in your rant—the new recruit?"

"Joey's been a good friend since high school." Lacey swallowed hard, not wanting to put her longtime friend in a compromising position with the Chief.

The phone rang and Chief took the call. While he sputtered into the receiver of about fifty arrests made and a plethora of drugs seized at a Phish concert, Lacey read the recent crimes listed on the white board; one officer sustained a broken ankle and a broken wrist at the concert. There was also a rash of car bashing incidents where senior citizens were forced off icy secondary roads during inclement winter weather. Several victims were seriously injured. One eighty-four-year old woman died from her injuries at Samaritan Hospital.

Lacey thought of Gran Likoudis' rosary group who met every Wednesday in all types of weather. She was sure Gran and her friends would not heed her warning about these heinous crimes but she would try to impress upon them this was serious enough for them to take notice.

Chief hung up the phone and stood up, exhibiting his 6'5" frame. "I did not like the way Santora intimidated you at the ceremony. If he becomes a threat to your training, your future job with the force, to your family—I want to know immediately."

In a tone that was both worried and hostile, Lacey said, "I thought I was done with Vinnie Santora. If I come across evidence proving he's responsible for any of these crimes," she nodded at the white board, "I'll let you know. I hear things on the street."

Chief buzzed the intercom and requested a restraining order.

Lacey cringed; this was not what she expected for this meeting. She had hoped it was about her future goals, but the meeting had taken a dismal turn into the mistakes she had hoped to leave long behind her.

Molly breezed in with a form. Chief scrawled his signature across the paper and handed it to Lacey. "That's a restraining order against Santora to include protection for you and your family. It's a flimsy piece of paper. Remember, you're a rookie, not an officer. I want information from you, not action. Rely on our men for reinforcement if anything problematic happens."

"And women," Lacey dared to flash a unified look at Molly. She tucked the order into her shoulder bag. As she went out the door, she nearly bumped into Joey McGrath, who was heading into Chief's office. Lacey felt her shoulders sag, although she tried to regain composure before anyone caught the slight slump. After the meeting, seeing McGrath was not comforting, but rather disconcerting. Vinnie Santora was already casting a shadow onto her future at the police academy.

CHAPTER 3

VINNIE SANTORA

'To expect bad men not to do wrong is madness'

– *Marcus Aurelius*

The sign read: Dr. Micah Masters, Specialist in Women's Health. Inside the second floor of the derelict skyscraper located on a Washington Heights side street in Manhattan, the dingy reception area was three-quarters full.

Nervous young pregnant patients waited alone or with a companion to be examined by an avant-garde doctor or, if in labor, to give birth. No one was aware of the turmoil going on in the inner chambers of the clinic.

"Please . . . someone help me. I don't want to do this. I don't want to do this. Where's ma?" A fifteen-year-old girl pleaded as she was wheeled on an unstable gurney down the cold, dreary hallway lined with clinical rooms on both sides. The grubby male attendant sharply turned the gurney to the left, paying no heed to the pleas of the young patient about to give birth. He slammed the base of the gurney into a heavy steel door opening into a room lit by blinding white lights. There was an eruption of activity between a doctor and two nurses anxious to do their part in birthing a newborn infant.

Twenty minutes later, a keen wail penetrated the dismal space inside the sweltering delivery room. The exhausted teen attempted to raise her sweat-drenched head. "I want to see my baby," she pleaded weakly. "A boy or girl?"

"Boy," said the nurse attendant. "7 pounds, 1 . . ."

The corpulent doctor who looked more like a professional wrestler than a physician snapped impatiently, "Just clean up the mess, nurse, and swaddle the lad."

The teen mom kicked her legs and flailed her arms causing insurmountable pain. "Give him to me. I want to hold my baby." Her frightened eyes filled with tears. She felt a prick of a needle and then slipped into oblivion.

"Is the baby ready?" Doc Masters asked while wiping his bloody hands on a filthy towel. He tossed the towel into an overflowing laundry bin. The nurse nodded and held the perfect Italian newborn in her arms.

Doctor hastily scratched out an invoice for $6000.00. He scoffed while handing it to her, "not many blond, blue eyed kids coming through the system lately. They are the ones to fetch a hefty price." He tossed the pen onto a chaotic desk. "Take him to the back door and hand him over to Mr. and Mrs. Nicholas Santora. Then get ready for the next delivery. We have nine today barring no complications."

Four years later . . . an adorable dark-haired boy climbed on monkey bars in the gated neighborhood park while his nanny, Louella, watched over him. He'd been playing with several playmates when he stopped suddenly, as he did so often lately, and tugged at the front of his designer jeans and scratched his crotch.

While gossiping with another nanny, Louella Cassidy, a short, stocky young woman who recently emigrated from Ireland with proper credentials, jumped up and scurried over to her charge. "Vinnie, don't touch yourself like that, please. It's rude! Your friends will laugh at you and tease you something wicked."

Vinnie burst out crying and continued to scratch himself. "But it hurts me bad, Lo'ella." Tears streamed down his face.

"Let's go home. We've got to get to the bottom of this." She grabbed his arm and they headed in the direction of an Upper East Side apartment complex, home to Vinnie Santora and his parents, Nicholas and Barbara.

"Nic, I had to let Louella go today," Barbara Santora said to her husband as he shook out the newspaper he was reading intently. He raised his eyes to her as if to dismiss the topic of Louella

Cassidy. "So . . . get another nanny for cripes sake, Barbara." He stretched out the syllables of her name, exasperated. "Are you totally helpless?"

"Nic, listen to me for once." Barbara was not going to be intimidated by her authoritative husband this time. She sensed trouble brewing for her sorry excuse of a family and she intended to stop it. Nic's sick games with Vinnie were becoming obvious and risky. "Louella became suspicious and accused someone at the daycare of sexually abusing Vinnie."

"And you couldn't quash the rumor? You're of no use to me, Barbara. Beautiful but toxic." He shook the paper again.

Shaking all over with browbeaten rage, Barbara erupted. "The nurse at the day care center called me today. Mrs. Atkin told me in no uncertain terms Vinnie is being sexually abused by an adult and she is reporting it to the Guardians office. We can expect to be interviewed immediately. There will be an investigation."

Nic's eyes grew large and round as a contemplative look passed over his dark, handsome features. His lips turned up in a devious smile as he said, "An investigation you say? Guardians' office? He dropped the paper to the floor and leaned his head back in his chair. "Don't worry; I'll take care of the Guardians' Office with a phone call. Oh, and Barbara, it's time to adopt another baby. A girl this time."

"Oh Nic, no."

"Oh yes, Barbara."

The years from ages four to eleven lacked coherence for young Vinnie Santora. His father was obsessed with the new baby girl, Emily, who came into the family one fine spring day. Vinnie recalled the tulips, daffodils and hyacinths blooming in Central Park and spending idyllic afternoons playing baseball with a select group of friends. As time passed, Vinnie could tell by the baby's actions and facial expressions she was terrorized by their father as he once had been. The physical pain she endured, and the fear written over her tiny face when she set eyes upon their father was pitiable to see. He sympathized with his baby sister and at the same time felt relieved the days of his father's attentions on him were over.

When Emily turned four and went to pre-school, a new baby brother arrived. Emilio Santora became the apple of his father's eye.

Vinnie's relationship with his mother was relatively close although he did not see her often. At an early age he recognized the fact his mother feared his father as much as he and his siblings did. She was abused mentally and not physically. When his father realized mother and son had bonded, he did everything in his power to separate them. Shortly thereafter Vinnie made a pact with his mother and it was a secret to this day.

Nanny's A, B, C, D, and E became the essential part of the Santora children's lives. When a nanny suspected abuse, they were let go immediately. In some cases, Vinnie supposed they were paid off with an expensive gift to keep quiet.

It was age twelve when Vinnie met Mr. Z. Mr. Z was a guidance counselor at Colton Private School. Vinnie never did know Mr. Z's full name. Vinnie was a boarder at the prestigious Colton School located in upper Manhattan. Vinnie felt enormous relief being away from his dysfunctional home and family. He made friends easily in 7th grade. He discovered a talent he never knew he had; he was a natural leader and peers gravitated to him.

His chief admirer was Mr. Z who disregarded school rules and regulations by taking Vinnie out to lunch at a nearby Mickey

D's where they chomped on cheeseburgers, French fries and diet cokes. With half an hour to spare during lunchtime, they parked in St. Joseph's Catholic Church's parking lot. There, Mr. Z made Vinnie's body feel good whereas his father's touches were threatening and creepy. Mr. Z was a funny guy whose jokes made Vinnie laugh. Mr. Z was the 'greatest.'

After Vinnie graduated from Colton School, his father had plans for him to go on to Medical School to become a doctor. When at home for a period of a month, he felt lost without his habitual routine at the exclusive school including camaraderie with classmates and time spent with Mr. Z. He barely knew his younger brother and two sisters. They were aloof and subdued. Even though he knew the reason for their reticence he was too wrapped up in his own problems to care.

He snapped one day and threw the plans to become a Specialist Physician in his father's face. That night he left the cold, mausoleum of a dwelling and the draconian family, and merged into the street life of Manhattan where he felt he belonged at last.

"Vinnie, how many years have you been *linchpin* in the Troy crime scene?" Starr Ellis asked the young rolling stone reclining on a soft leather couch in her Troy, New York apartment. It was a trendy urban flat she had moved into four years ago. Located in the central Troy district on Congress Street where all pathways led to voguish stores for shopping, eclectic restaurants, churches, and museums.

She could do without the Troy Police Station in her neighborhood. Some of her activities were not conducive to the law and it made her uncomfortable when a police officer called her by name and waved. Seconds later he would eye her suspiciously. At those times she reminded herself the nature of an officer was to be wary of everyone. Take into consideration, Lacey O'Dunn, a former collaborator in the drug scene and once an ally to her and Vinnie. Lacey was currently clean and in the process of becoming a cop. Former teammates, Joey McGrath and Greg Conners, were also becoming rookie cops. However, they tended to slip every now and then. The drugs Vinnie sold so readily were a magnet to each of them.

"I'm twenty-nine; I'd say it's about ten years since I moved out of stinking, rotten Manhattan. Did I ever tell you I was a black market baby?" Vinnie asked with a hint of sarcasm. "I never knew my real mother and father. Vincent and Barbara bought me and my siblings from a hack doctor. Why the questions now?" Vinnie kept his eyes on the epoch MAD comic book he was reading.

"Just because . . ." Starr said distractedly. "Hey man, I need a Xanax. I'm jittery."

Vinnie tossed a bottle of pills to her. The bottle landed at her bare feet. As she leaned over to grab the pills, she felt dizzy and nearly toppled over.

"Take it easy on the drugs, Starr. You're popping way too many. I'm getting too well-known at Troy Police Headquarters. I'm at the top of Troy's finest wanted list." He sneered. "Sleazebag Chief Ringwood's barking at his men to round me up. If that happened, I would be Ringwood's trophy."

Starr erupted into a coughing fit and broke into a clammy sweat. "Damn these pills. They give me hot flashes and headaches. I need a glass of ice-cold water and food. I haven't eaten at all today. Vinnie?"

Santora looked at Starr with malice in his eyes. "Since when have I become your nurse?" He pulled his long-limbed self from the couch and stomped into the kitchen. He poured a glass of ice water and brought it over to her. Deep in his pocket he fingered a silver pill he called Silver Ice. It was going to be introduced into the drug market eventually. Before it could be sold to users, he needed to find several guinea pigs. He hesitated and shoved it into a pill container. Now was not the time to make Starr a guinea pig. He did not want to deal with a bad reaction if she was inclined to have one. Once a raven-haired beauty, dark circles now encircled Starr's faded brown eyes. Her formerly flawless skin was blotchy with unsightly eruptions and her 5' 5" frame looked skeletal. She was twenty-six but she looked forty.

"Clean yourself up, woman. We're going out to dinner."

Starr raised her head and grimaced. "Where?" There was a guarded edge to her voice. Usually, they settled for a take-out meal at a nearby diner.

"Yoshi's. Will you hurry up?" Vinnie was hastily changing into fresh clothes. A tee shirt, black hoodie, and blue jeans.

"Isn't that Lacey O'Dunn's favorite restaurant? She usually goes there early on Tuesdays for a take-out meal she shares with her grandmother. What if she isn't there this week?"

"Then we'll go the week after or the following week. You're a smart girl, Starr. We'll catch up with her and her precious gran sometime and I'll throttle them." Vinnie spat out sarcastically.

"She'll think you're stalking her," Starr said worriedly, attempting to brush tangles out of her hair.

"That's the idea, my sweetness."

CHAPTER 4

EXPOSED

Knowing what you need to do to improve your life takes wisdom. Pushing yourself to do it takes courage.

*Mel Robbins Words to Live By,
Hoda Kotb with Jane Lorenzini*

The next morning, as Lacey left her new studio apartment to attend the police academy training session, her cell phone rang. Caller ID showed it was Gran Likoudis. She backed into the kitchen, not pleased with the thought of spending another evening socializing, even with comfy Gran. Every week since her recovery from drugs, Gran made it her business to have a sit-down dinner with Lacey to make sure that Lacey felt supported. If Gran would be honest about her intentions, she was probably making sure that Lacey was still sober and drug-free, which was easier to ensure with a face-to-face meeting.

"Lacey, I'm making a roast for dinner. Can you come?" Gran Likoudis' fragile voice wheezed. "I won't take no for an answer. The roast will be done at 5:30. Will that suit you?"

Lacey rubbed her forehead as if her headache would magically disappear. There was no way out. "Yes, Gran, it will." The upside to this minor annoyance was that Gran made a mouth-watering roast, so she was sure to have one amazing, warm meal this week.

"Good. I was beginning to think my granddaughter was blowing me off like my daughter and son-in-law."

It dawned on Lacey that it was possible these dinners were more for Gran and less about her sobriety than she'd first realized.

Lacey relaxed. "Silly Gran."

"I need to go to the store for bread and bananas. Do you need anything?" Gran asked. "And by the way, next week I promise to have dinner at your new apartment. My treat . . . a Japanese dinner from Yoshi's Restaurant."

Lacey perked up. She anticipated showing off her new apartment to her grandmother and paused to look out the window at the falling snow. Sleet was expected to follow, and soon, the roads would be unpredictable. She fought down panic recalling the white board in Chief's office: *No. 3 – A rash of car bashing incidents. Senior citizens forced off icy secondary roads.* Lacey's protective streak kicked in.

"Gran, I'll shop for you and drop the groceries off on my lunch break. You shouldn't be driving in this weather."

"I won't be gone any longer than I have to. You drive carefully and come tonight with a big appetite." Gran was fiercely guarded when it came to her independence. Many of her friends had been tucked away, safe, and secure, in nursing homes by family that visited occasionally. Gran refused to seem like she needed the same level of help that her friends had exhibited before being forced from their homes and into assisted living.

"I'm looking forward to your dinner," Lacey replied, unable to shake the concern that her grandmother insisted on shopping herself, "but I wish you would stay put in this bad weather."

"I appreciate your concern, Lacey, but I'm still capable of driving in all types of weather." There was the stubborn old woman who wouldn't take no for an answer.

"At least stay on the main roads. Car bumpers are attacking unsuspecting drivers." She described recent activities hoping to deter Gran from gallivanting around on back roads. Lacey would never forgive herself if she didn't at least try to keep Gran safe.

"I can defend myself from the baddies. I carry mace in the car."

"Gran, mace isn't going to stop a car basher from hitting the backside of your car." Lacey rolled her eyes; she knew it would be useless to argue with her grandmother.

Lacey reached for the last knob of the rock-climbing wall. She felt satisfied; she had energy left and could keep on going. Months of conditioning for training had left her limbs hungry for the sting of exertion. She was outperforming her peers with ease, and she secretly hoped that information would make it back to Chief's ears to redeem her from the Vinnie Santora ordeal.

A shrill voice echoed in the Police Academy gym, calling out her name. A sigh escaped as Lacey imagined another chastising conversation, like the one from the day before. She had no intentions of cutting training short to engage in another question-and-answer session about her past acquaintances and pressed her chin to her chest while staring down at Molly's upturned face.

"Lacey, you've a phone call." Molly raised a cell phone over her head, extending toward Lacey, instead of demanding that she come down.

"Can't it wait?" Lacey gasped.

Molly shook her head back and forth, a firm dissent, "Your mother says it's urgent."

Lacey felt a sudden chill come over her. "Please God, not Gran." Her intuition was rarely wrong.

She swayed backwards and then tightened her grip on the faux rocks. Four trainees held a rope as she gripped it and eased herself downwards. She bumped her knee on a sharp edge on the descent. Pain shot through her, and she bit down on her lip before planting her feet on the hard floor, catching her balance.

Lacey took the phone from Molly and limped to the edge of the gym, listening to her mother's frantic words: "Gran's friend, Francis Carson, was in an automobile accident this morning. Dad and I are at the hospital. Gran's staying with Francis until the family arrives."

Lacey pulled a towel off a rack on the wall. She wiped sweat off her face and arms, and blood off her knee while heading to the locker room. She quizzed her mother, "Do you know what happened? What road was she on?"

Without waiting for an answer, Lacey continued,

"I'll be at the hospital as soon as I can. Is Francis going to be all right?"

"Doctor Stevens is evaluating her now," her mother said, and in the next breath warned, "Take care, Lacey. The roads are treacherous."

Lacey's mind began to race. Was this another incident that would make it onto Chief Ringwood's office board? She had been warned to let the experienced officers do their job, without inserting herself, but Lacey had a knack for wanting to be the one that figured it all out. She hadn't read all the Nancy Drew, Sherlock Holmes, and Agatha Christie books for nothing! With Francis being a life-long family friend, Lacey knew that she could get some answers before anyone from the department suspected that she was up to something.

In a record time of twenty minutes, Lacey passed through the rotating doors of the Samaritan Hospital. She hurried toward the waiting elevator, entered the sanitized chamber, and rode up three floors. Her parents were huddled together outside ICU, which seemed like a bad omen. "Where's Gran?" Lacey's voice was tense.

Her father squeezed her arm when she approached. "She's in the room with Francis and Doctor Stevens. We've learned that Francis's vitals are good, except for an erratic heartbeat. She's delirious due to a head injury, but it's expected to be a temporary condition." Hunter O'Dunn paused and added wearily, "And, she has a broken ankle from the impact."

"Poor dear lady. Gran must be beside herself. She and Francis are inseparable. Tell me what happened." Lacey sat down on a sagging couch next to her mother in the waiting room.

Nita Likoudis O'Dunn clenched an unlit cigarette between her fingertips. "It appears that Francis slid on a patch of black ice at the intersection of Route 23 and Cobbs Hollow Road. Her car went down an embankment and hit a tree. She's lucky a broken ankle was the worst of her injuries. A trucker saw the car in the ditch and dialed 911. When help arrived, they brought her to the hospital in an ambulance. Gran was asked by Francis's daughter to stay with her until the family arrives. Gran called us, and we came right away."

"Francis shouldn't have been driving in icy conditions," Hunter piped up. "Ma shouldn't drive on these roads either." Lacey nodded in agreement, remembering the conversation she and Gran had earlier that morning.

Nita scoffed, "If you live in this area, you have to drive on bad winter roads or become a recluse. I don't intend to do that, and I assure you neither does Ma." Lacey felt a grin tug at the corners of her lips, recognizing that the females of the family all had the same stubborn, independent demeanor. Despite trying to be a voice of reason to Gran, Lacey had to appreciate that she followed in the footsteps of strong women who wouldn't take no for an answer. This stemmed from her new position with the police department and her desire to show that she had what it takes to be a tough officer, in spite of her past.

Lacey stood up and faced her parents. "It's not driving on wintry roads that concerns me."

They stared at her blankly.

"What concerns you besides the roads?" Hunter pressed.

"A car basher." She told them about the latest criminal activities being investigated by the police. She left out the part of being told to leave well enough alone while in training. She didn't need her parents worrying about her blooming career while Francis was still being fixed up from a wreck, but her hope was that the new information would enable them to strong arm Gran into staying off the still unknown path of the car basher.

A sudden dawning came across Nita's face. "That's what Ma was rambling about. She insisted Francis kept repeating the car was struck from behind. Deliberately!" Nita waved her hand. "Ma said she plans on inciting vigilantes among her rosary group to search for the baddies."

"I told Gran about the car basher to keep her off icy roads," Lacey expelled a deep breath, "not to get a posse together from the church." She sighed. "Whatever you do, don't let her out of your sight. I'm going to see if the report on Francis's accident is ready and available."

CHAPTER 5

UNLIKE CONNECTIONS

Fall seven times and standup eight

Japanese Proverb

At the police station, Molly was not at her desk. Lacey did not wish to disturb Chief Ringwood behind a closed door, so she slipped behind Molly's desk and rifled through papers in the file bin. One document in the middle of the ingoing pile caught her eye.

"What are you doing?" a stout woman who resembled Molly Baines snapped. "I had to go to the loo. Couldn't you wait?" She slid her pocketbook on a ledge beneath the desk.

Lacey waved her hand. "Sorry, but I'm in a hurry. I need to see Francis Carson's accident report." With frustration in her voice, she asked, "Where's Molly? Are you a relative? You resemble her."

"Molly and I are fraternal twins. I'm Mabel Marks. I'm filling in for my sister while she's at a dentist appointment." The woman glared, acting tough as Molly was pleasant and cooperative.

"Why are you in a hurry to see the report without going through protocol?" Mabel narrowed her eyes in an intimidating manner.

"Francis Carson is a family friend. You weren't at the desk, so I took the liberty of looking for the accident report. Surely, you don't mind." Lacey tried to get in Mabel's good graces by seeming helpful, instead of appearing to be a snoop that crossed boundaries.

"I do mind, and I'll report you to the Chief because of your actions." Lacey winced; this was not how she wanted day two of being in the department to go.

"Tell me, was this accident due to the car basher?" Lacey pressed forward.

With a deliberately cool tone and slanted eyes, Mabel answered, "You're persistent, Miss Lacey. A word of warning . . . don't get ahead of yourself, you're not on the force yet. Chief's got the report on his desk. You want to see it, feel free to ask him." Mabel plunked down in her seat and turned her computer on, signaling that she had other things to occupy her time.

Lacey zipped and unzipped her shoulder bag out of nervousness. "His door is closed. I don't want to barge in."

Mabel turned away from Lacey dismissively. "Damn, the phone." She picked up the vibrating receiver and her caustic voice said, "Central Police, Call Receiving Officer."

Lacey yawned as she drove two miles to Dom's Garage. The two-story concrete building was located at one corner of an intersection, adjacent to a shopping mall, a garden center, and a historic cemetery reputed to be haunted. Lacey suspected Dom's Garage closed at five in daylight to escape any late-night visitors from the cemetery. She smiled, imagining cousin Dom bee-lining to his truck.

Lacey pulled alongside a black Cadillac with more rust than paint. She stretched and clomped through slush and melting ice to a warped side door. Grabbing the handle through gloved hands, she wrinkled her nose ahead of the working garage smell she knew was about to hit her in the face.

Heat washed over her when she went inside the garage reeking of gas and oil. She stomped snow off her boots and tossed her parka over a sagging, overstuffed chair. This was a place she felt comfortable, and she expected to get the answers she needed without an interrogation from Chief or any other officer. She was convinced Francis's accident was caused by the car bashers. She was taken aback when Molly's sister, Mabel Marks, would not reveal to her the probable cause of Francis's accident. Code of behavior, she surmised, realizing she had a lot to learn as a rookie cop. She would have to control her ambitious personality.

A tall, lanky mechanic with curly, dark hair tied into a ponytail was bent over the hood of a red Mazda in a stall. Dom Menos held a diagnostic machine in his hand.

"What could possibly be wrong with that car? It looks brand new," Lacey commented.

Dom scratched his head. "I'm trying to find what's shorting out the engine. What brings you here, cousin? Let me guess. You need a tank of gas. Well, you haven't paid me for the last two fill-ups, so the answer is no."

"I need to know your evaluation on the cars Chief Ringwood had towed here after six or more recent accidents."

Dom looked at Lacey, his dark eyes telling her to back off. "I report to the chief, not you, Lacey." He ducked his head beneath the hood.

"Dom, I know about the cars being bumped off the road. I suspect Francis Carson's car is one of them."

Dom pulled away from the hood. "Francis, the fluffy-haired lady who made hot fudge sundaes when we visited her as kids? That Francis?" Dom had grown up with the same loyalty factors Lacey had, and she was relieved that the name dropping had obtained his interest.

Lacey nodded. "Gran Likoudis' good friend. Gran's with her at the hospital. Francis is banged up pretty good."

Dom wiped his hands on a gritty cloth and tossed it into a bin. "Lacey, I'm sorry to hear about Francis, but you're not wearing a badge . . . yet. I'm not going to jeopardize my career, or yours, by giving out information that belongs to the Chief of Police."

Lacey folded her arms, feeling the adolescent rivalry grow in her chest. "Fine, I'll tell Gran there's nothing to be done until the police get their act together. She'll take off with her weekly rosary posse, and they'll take matters into their own hands."

"Meaning?" Dom pointed his eyes at Lacey.

"Like, trying to find out who's bumping old people off slick, icy roads and doing something about it themselves."

Dom rubbed his nose. "That'd be crazy to do something like that." He also knew Gran wouldn't leave this alone, just like the woman standing before him.

Lacey's eyes flickered. "Tell me what car Francis was driving." Dom waved her toward the back door. They went into the frigid air to a back lot where broken cars waited to be repaired. Walking past four crumpled vehicles they came upon a green Subaru Forester and a white Honda Civic.

Dom brushed snowflakes off his shoulders. "Francis's car is the Forester."

Lacey slowly circled both vehicles taking in the damage done to each car. "There's a definite pattern." She pointed to identical indentations appearing several inches above the back bumpers of the Forester and Civic. "It's as if . . ."

"Why am I not surprised you are here busy-body O'Dunn," Chief Ringwood barked. Lacey and Dom both jumped at the Irish baritone of his voice. He sloshed through the lot and came over to them. Angry and out of patience, he said, "You were written up once today for going through papers on a clerk's desk, which is a serious offense, and now you're interfering with an investigation. One more conflict and you're done, Miss O'Dunn."

"Chief, I have the right to view Francis Carson's car. I know her personally. Anyone can view the car," she said testily. Dom had been concerned about this very thing and now it was playing out right in front of him. His beautiful, twinkle-eyed cousin had brains and courage he wished he possessed.

"Don't take it any further, I warn you. There's no shortcut to being a cop. You have to be trained like everyone else." He turned to Dom after motioning Lacey to leave.

She scurried toward the door, hoping she wouldn't hear from Dom later that he had also been chewed out by the Chief.

"Have you any news from the lab?"

"I should have the report sometime this afternoon or tomorrow morning. Then, I can tell you more about the paint color and model of the other vehicle." Dom stomped his numb feet.

"I want the information as soon as you have it. A maniac is on the loose, causing six accidents, one fatal." Chief Ringwood was on a mission to stop more fatalities from happening. He knew the investigations had to be thorough and seamless to get the conviction to stick. The last thing he needed was a rookie getting evidence thrown out before he even had a suspect.

"Tell the desk to patch you through to my cell as soon as you have some answers." Before Chief Ringwood turned and trudged back to his cruiser he cautioned the mechanic, "A word of warning; don't give information to Miss Busybody before you give it to me, or you will no longer have the business of Central Police."

Dom almost saluted the Chief but nodded his head instead. "Yes, sir."

Dom thought of Francis as one of the victims. Alone in the lot for a moment, he stared at the indentations on the Forester and the Civic. It was the same pattern as on the other four cars. He heard Lacey walking back to him after Chief had been gone for several minutes. He shook his head back and forth when she said, "It's as if the Devil bumped the cars from behind and the drivers lost control, sending the cars off the road."

Dom turned his head to the side to look at her, after all, he was the one doing this job long enough to understand unusual patterns in the bodies of cars. He was also the one analyzing the vehicles after they had been wrecked.

"Let the professionals do their job, Lacey. Will you please?" he shook his head dourly.

Lacey's brain needed time to process. She looked down at her watch. "Oh, I'm going to be late for dinner with Gran. I'll catch up with you later."

CHAPTER 6

DISCLOSURE

"Entrusting one's life is not the same as opening up one's soul."

Muriel Barbery, *The Elegance of the Hedgehog*

The sun was fading on the horizon, creating an eerie blue dusk when Lacey pulled in front of the Samaritan Hospital. Since Gran had been at the hospital with Francis for the last few hours, Lacey had convinced her to put their original dinner plans on hold. She leaned over and opened the car door. With obvious stiffness, Gran Likoudis slid into the passenger seat.

"Did you pick up the two Number sevens at Yoshi's Restaurant?" Gran sniffed the air. "They smell delicious. I will reimburse you when we get to your apartment."

Lacey nodded as she pulled the car out of the angled passenger slot onto the main road.

Gran listened closely as her granddaughter spoke.

"Regrettably, I ran into Vinnie Santora and Starr Ellis at the restaurant. It was an awkward moment on my part, but it didn't seem to bother Vinnie." Lacey pulled strands of her long blond hair away from her neck and lowered the heating knob. "I'm afraid Starr's playing my former role as Vinnie's string-puppet," she said more to herself than to her grandmother. Lacey tapped the restraining order in her jacket pocket with a new respect for Chief Ringwood. He had the foresight to see that Vinnie may be a continual threat to her. "How's Francis now?" She pulled her thoughts away from Vinnie Santora.

Gran smiled. "Can't keep the old girl down. She'll be cheering her grandson's basketball team tomorrow evening."

"Glad to hear that." Lacey sighed.

"Any word on the car bashers?" Gran fidgeted with her seat belt.

With one hand gripping the steering wheel, Lacey reached over and slid the clamp into its slot.

"Nothing at all."

She turned onto a side road which led to her apartment complex and parked the car in a reserved space. "It's frustrating," Gran said as she climbed out of the car and balanced herself before walking forward. She shook off Lacey's arm and took baby steps along the sanded walkway on her own. Suddenly, she stopped walking and a low whistle escaped her lips. "Hubba, hubba."

Lacey raised her head but saw only a large shadow gripping a leash restricting a small barking Pothound. The shadow and dog were standing in front of the ice machine. "Who do you see, Gran?" Her brain sent out a warning signal.

"The good-looking Chief of Police. I remember seeing him at your swearing-in ceremony. He gave an excellent speech. Look, he's coming toward us. Oh, and look at that cute Potcake," she said gleefully.

A tall hunk of a man dressed in silk athletic shorts, a gray tee-shirt with a POLICE logo, and barefoot in sandals, sauntered down the walkway carrying a full ice bucket. In the lead was a tan Bahamian Pothound with pointy ears.

"Chief!" Lacey called out.

Chief Ringwood looked surprised.

"Lacey? Well, well," he smiled crisply. "We meet again under more pleasant circumstances. You do get around, Miss O'Dunn."

"How nice," Gran gushed. "The two of you not only work together but you're neighbors."

"You live here?" Lacey blathered. She felt incredibly ludicrous.

"For the past five years in the corner townhouse."

"In the high rent district." Gran clapped her hands. "Lacey's in a studio apartment." She eyed her granddaughter, wondering why she looked uncomfortable and tongue-tied. "It's a perfect situation for now. Lacey?"

"There's nothing for me to add, Gran." Lacey's Irish skin blushed a deep rose. She hoped Gran was not playing matchmaker so obviously.

Chief shifted the ice bucket to his other hand as well as switching the dog leash. "Here, let me carry a couple of your bags." He relieved her of the aromatic food and sniffed the air. "Something smells good."

Gran's eyes widened. "You should have dinner with us. It's Japanese." Gran's voice hit a sweet crescendo on the final two words in her attempt to tempt him with the style of food. Gran was old school enough to know the way to a man's heart was through his stomach.

"Thanks, ma'am, another time. I've got work to do and this little critter wants a treat. Besides, I'm freezing out here. My place is warm but I like to pretend it's summer while I work out."

Lacey unlocked the door and reached around the doorframe to switch on the lights. Chief stood with his back against the door and let the women enter, proving he was as chivalrous as he was married to his work.

Gran gave Chief an analytical look and said, "I picture you with a German Sheppard or a Golden Retriever; not this sweet little pup."

Chief nodded his head. "It's a long story and I'll make it short. If I didn't take him in, he'd be ground up for cat food by now. I rescued Foxy during a criminal case we were working on. He's tough and loyal."

Gran blanched at the thought of an endearing dog like Foxy meeting a violent end. She quickly changed the subject. "Have you solved the car bashing crimes? My good friend is a victim."

Lacey felt a prickle of heat trail across her neck as Chief stared at her. She shouldn't have told Gran what was official police information, but she had to warn her of the recent car bashings. Especially when her good friend, Francis was now a possible victim.

Gran went on to explain Francis's accident and how her rosary group were willing to search the snowy roads for suspicious activity.

Chief's eyes strayed from Lacey to her grandmother. In the bright light, Chief looked tired. "No one wants to catch these lawbreakers more than I do. The cases remain unsolved . . . but not for long."

In Chief Ringwood fashion, his husky voice grew stern as he warned, "Ma'am, I need no outside help. My officers are working around the clock to catch these bashers." He eyed Lacey and concluded, "Professionalism is desperately needed to catch these devils on black ice."

Gran's eyes widened and knew her technique was defeated this time. She wanted to quiz Chief further on the cases of car bashing.

She maintained her dignity by praising, "Lacey, this apartment's perfect for you. I'll make a pot of coffee and serve the food." She gave a cheeky smile to the chief and walked away in a dismissive gesture. "Nice to see you Chief Ringwood. Perhaps another time you can join us for dinner. We'll celebrate after the car bashers are caught and in jail."

Lacey raised her hands in a helpless gesture.

Chief winked and then turned and made an exit down the well-lit path. Lacey's eyes followed him, unsure how to deal with the thoughts that swirled in her mind. He was attractive, career-driven—which was incredibly appealing to her—and he lived in the same complex as her. Lacey pushed enticing thoughts away and proceeded to focus on the food and Gran's company.

Lacey stopped at the Craft Center of Troy after a heavy training schedule the next day. She had promised to pick up a handmade shawl for Gran Likoudis to give as a get-well gift to Francis. She was surprised to see Starr Ellis standing before a mirror, tweaking her recently colored and trimmed punk-red hair, and putting on lipstick.

Starr's eyes were smudged and showed the strain of a long night. Lacey felt a pang of pity; she remembered those days. Gratitude for being out of that lifestyle also welled up inside Lacey, and she appreciated the free will she was experiencing.

Slouched in a chair, out of Lacey's line of vision, was Vinnie Santora. He flew out of the seat and clipped over to Lacey. "Just the piece of crap I want to see." He grabbed her arms and held them hard. Lacey's heart started racing faster than her brain could process his proximity. She had missed his presence on her initial scan of her surroundings. When fight or flight kicked in, Lacey realized she wanted to do both in the same moment, and she couldn't decide if that was a good sign or a bad one.

Outwardly, Lacey remained calm, inwardly, she was falling apart. "Take your hands off me," she said evenly. Her tone shocked her, as she realized that the turmoil inside wasn't translating externally.

Vinnie pressed harder. His dilated eyes told the story. He was on heroin. "Tell Chief Pig to stay out of my business. Since the two of you are an item—"

Lacey shook her head. "There's no truth to that." She attempted to pull away, but she did not have enough strength. A weird phenomenon of drug addicts was their strength. When they were high, it was superhuman.

"I'm not car bashing," he raged. His eyes narrowed and his mouth twisted savagely. "Tell Chief Pig to look in his own camp."

His accusation that an officer could be guilty sent shivers down Lacey's back. There were case studies where first responders created emergencies to respond to, and Lacey made a mental note to pay attention to her peers and their interest in the cases. Off the top of her head, she couldn't think of anyone besides Chief and herself that were personally invested in figuring these car bashing cases out.

She prepared to knee him when a soft tinkling of a bell announced customers were entering the store. Two middle aged women stared at Lacey and Vinnie.

"Shannon," one nervous woman said, "perhaps we'll browse another time."

"It's all right to shop, ladies," Starr smiled sweetly. "It's a lover's quarrel. The gentleman is leaving." She glared at Vinnie. He took his cue while staring daggers into Lacey.

Vinnie stomped through the door while Lacey went in search for her grandmother's gift for Francis. Lacey had made up her mind to show no fear and continue with business as usual. After all, how could she become the best in blue if she could be easily intimidated by the likes of Vinnie Santora? She had not threatened him with the restraining order this time.

Starr stumbled over an apology as she bagged a few items Lacey picked up before ordering the shawl and rang up the charge. "Sorry Vinnie was a little off today." She bit down on her lip. "But you were his squeeze once; you know how it is." Lacey realized how difficult it must be for Starr to look at her as the past girlfriend while she was trying to be the current one. Little did Starr know that it was the drugs and alcohol that made Lacey susceptible to Vinnie's clutches, not by any merit or character he possessed.

"Looks like he's tiring you out; you look beat." Lacey's eyes were full of compassion as she said this to Starr; she knew the lifestyle well enough to know that Starr was stuck on stupid for now. When she sobered up and got free, she would look back at the situation through eyes of regret and remorse, much like Lacey did now.

Starr brightened, attempting to cast doubt on the statement Lacey had made. "Vinnie's a lot of fun. I love the guy." She hesitated and said, "I'm sorry for the scene last night at Yoshi's. Vinnie gets carried away with the moment. You know the routine . . . once you belong to Vinnie, he thinks he owns you forever."

Lacey refrained from commenting. Her eyes went interestedly from Starr to an empty space in the parking lot. "Where's your red truck?"

"My pride and joy got beat up a little. Tough winter driving, you know. A fender bender. My brother's repairing the bumper for me."

Lacey stared at Starr in an uncomfortable silence. She was about to say something that flashed in her mind but thought better of it. She turned and left the store.

CHAPTER 7

THE OFFENDERS

Products of their circumstances.
Products of their decisions.

"Chief Ringwood, it's Dominick Menos from Dom's Garage. I have information about the accidents."

"Finally, a break. How soon can you get the report over to me?" Chief adjusted the phone to his ear while prioritizing messages. Two urgent memos glared at him.

"My cousin picked up the folder on her way to training this morning and dropped it off at your office minutes ago," Dom admitted sheepishly.

"Let's hear it from you," Chief said, exasperation in his deep brogue voice. "I'll read the report later." He made a mental note to chastise Lacey for overstepping her boundaries again. This seemed to be a pattern with her.

"The techy's lifted two types of paint off the damaged vehicles. A polyester red and a urethane silver topcoat. There's a third tint he can't make out yet, possibly black or hunter green. These colors and a one-inch gash turned up on the trunks of each damaged car. After the final lab report is in, we should be able to identify the colors and the types of vehicles."

"Thanks, Dom. From now on, you bring in the reports, not a third party for security reasons, understand?" Chief Ringwood needed to close the gap that Lacey kept finding between protocol and her own goals.

"Yes, sir." Dom kicked himself for not getting approval for the pickup beforehand. He didn't need to lose the department's business for sloppy paperwork issues. He made a mental note to put Lacey in her place *pronto*.

"Silver," Lacey repeated, her heart racing fast. Silver was the color found on Francis's car. She was mulling the fact over as she knocked loudly on Chief Ringwood's office door.

"Come in." It was a command, not an invitation.

She stepped inside, shocked to see his black eyebrows twitching above enraged eyes. She stared resolutely, warding off his scathing assessment by picturing him with hives on his face. It had worked in high school. She wasn't the type to employ the underwear tactic, that would make her giggle, and Chief's face was far too serious to laugh.

"Hey, you were in a good mood this morning at the gym. Why are you so angry?" At 5:00 A.M. that morning, at the housing complex gym, he had joked with her while they coincidently spent an hour doing spinning exercises. Lacey was trying to invoke his memory to lessen whatever was coming down the proverbial pipeline.

His voice snapped when he told her about his conversation with Dom at the garage. "You had no right to pick up the lab reports and deliver them to this office. That's official business and most likely you read them, because you can't help but insert yourself in things you have been warned to stay out of."

Lacey flushed from neck to forehead. It was a curse she had to live with due to her Irish heritage. She had absolutely read the reports.

Chief pulled a paper toward him, and he tapped his fingers on the desk. "According to this latest report, Nadia Likoudis patrols the back roads between Troy, New York and Bennington, Vermont with a senior rosary posse. This group is severely hampering the car bashing investigation of local and state authorities from two states." He snapped a pencil and tossed it across the room. "So, the apple doesn't land far from the family tree, does it?"

Lacey gave him a tight smile. "I apologize for my grandmother's actions. I'll have a talk with her." She coughed. "I see tomorrow's forecast is snow, sleet, and freezing rain. That means it will be a black ice day . . . A good day to put out some undercover cars and see if they get action."

Chief winced and continued in a voice ready to rant. To add to his misery, he was drowned out by a loud, clanging sound bouncing off a cinder block wall as a jailer closed a cell door. "It's none of your damn business what my team and I will be doing tomorrow, Ms. O'Dunn. I expect any progress will be made without outside interference. Understand?"

"Yes, Chief, I do." Lacey was already planning to see if she could borrow Gran's car for a couple of hours tomorrow. She would have to convince Gran not to tag along, but that shouldn't be too hard, given the excuse she planned to use. If all went well, no one would ever know what she was up to. If she ended up catching the culprit, so be it.

CHAPTER 8

ON THE ROAD AGAIN

Action always beats inaction.

Early next morning, Lacey raised the blinds and peered through her bedroom window. A mixture of snow, sleet, and freezing rain fell as the weatherperson had predicted the night before. She contemplated for a moment that it would be rousing to be in on the chase. The thought of Chief's grim face called to mind the fact that she was expected to go to training. Her impulsive actions were going to land her on the varied side of her career. She was leaning more toward the Plan B angle of becoming a private investigator.

Suddenly the phone rang. She picked up the receiver and heard the panic in her mother's voice. "Lacey, your grandmother has gathered her rosary posse and they're off to patrol the back roads."

"After I spoke with her last night, and she promised not to do this?" Lacey wailed.

Her mother gasped. "Sorry, Lacey, your father went to her house to try to talk sense to her. There was an argument. She's determined . . ."

Sighing out loud, Lacey could imagine how that conversation went down.

"Okay, calm down. I'll find her. Chief warned me yesterday not to interfere with this investigation. He said I would be walking out on my career. Blast, Gran." Lacey complained to her mother, playing up the innocence she did not have in this situation. She had also put together that Mom was now an alibi for why Lacey was missing training when she had been told not to interfere in the investigation.

Lacey knelt on the floor in her bedroom and rummaged through the hope chest at the foot of the bed. She was on a mission now, and it may cost her training to be a police officer. Under the circumstances, she felt she had no choice. Cogent thought did not come easily. It was time to assess the fact she was better suited to be a private detective akin to her ersatz uncle and her father's good friend, Tony Pastore. Uncle Tony had once been a Troy, New York cop. He left the force due to being held down by unreasonable political demands where the law and jack-ass politicians were concerned. He realized he could move further along the investigation process on his own. A light bulb suddenly turned on in Lacey's head. She imagined being free to bend rules as a P. I. following in Uncle Tony's footsteps.

After several minutes of searching through musty clothes, photo albums, and memorabilia, she leaned back on her heels and shook out a curly gray wig. She went over to the mirror and placed it on her head. She removed a silk scarf from a bureau drawer and tied it beneath her chin. She slipped into a long black coat, covering her tee shirt and jeans. Satisfied, she took her pocketbook and car keys with her. The only thing that could have made the disguise more complete was a wrinkled rubber face mask, like the ones kids wore on Halloween.

She drove the all-wheel drive vehicle down the main road about a mile and a half in slush and veered left off the highway onto ice-coated Route 23. She headed toward the intersection of Cobbs Hollow Road, barely avoiding a skid as the conditions worsened. The car basher would be out for certain if the road conditions continued this trend.

Her thoughts were on Grans Likoudis and the rosary posse. The roads were treacherous. Her hope was the group of old timers gave up the chase and went to their respective homes to settle in for a cup of tea and a card game of canasta or gin rummy. So far it was smooth sailing and there was no other vehicle in sight.

After five miles of tricky driving on icy roads, a red truck suddenly appeared at an intersection. The truck, which she was certain to be Starr's, eased to a stop and Lacey cautiously drove through the crossroads. She pushed back against the seat when in the rear-view mirror, she caught a glimpse of the truck drawing close behind her. Huge sunglasses and a black hood on the driver made her unable to make out any facial features. She watched in helpless shock as the truck charged forward and rammed her bumper.

With her heart hammering in her chest, Lacey navigated an icy curve. A blue car with flashing hazard lights came slowly around the bend. She beeped the horn, but the driver, gripping the steering wheel and paying attention to his side of the road ignored her and continued on.

The truck rammed her car again. This time, her vehicle spun in a half-circle in the middle of the road. With her throat constricted, she decided to act, reasoning that one slip-up could be deadly if the bumper car game continued.

A short distance down the road, Lacey drove the Subaru fast over a frost-heave she normally avoided this time of the year. She traveled this road often and knew it like the back of her hand. The Outback veered dangerously close to the edge of the pavement. She held tightly onto the steering wheel and the car fish-tailed to a stop.

The truck hammered over the frost-heave and lurched off-road, sliding head-long down a steep grade. An earth-shaking crash resounded as the truck rolled over and landed on its hood in a ditch.

Lacey sat riveted in the car, staring at the snow and sleet whirling in the flickering headlights. It was so dim and foggy she had switched the fog lights on. She jumped as the door flew open and a man in a black parka and cap pulled low on his forehead shoved her across the seat and hustled in beside her. Her piercing scream was followed by a feeling of intense liberation as she recognized Joey McGrath. "What 'th devil do you think you're doing, Lacey?" He snatched her wig and scarf off her head and tossed them into the back seat. "Are you crazy . . . are you hurt?"

With a powerful light shining from his Maglite flashlight she could see angst and relief on his face. She rubbed the back of her neck and with difficulty, she turned to face him. "I'm fine . . . just a bump on the head. Where did you come from, Joey?"

"Never mind me, I'm concerned about you." He removed his hat while in the warmth of the car and wiped perspiration off his forehead. "When the ambulance gets here, the medics will check you over." He shook his head. "I have to agree with Chief, Lacey. He was afraid you would pull a trick like this." He fumbled for tissues in his pocket and handed her one. Blood oozed from a cut on her forehead. "This was a dumb thing for you to do."

"What are you doing here, rookie? Isn't this job for the pros as Chief would say?" Lacey asked, a trace of irritation in her voice.

"Chief needed a couple of extras for this stake-out. He tapped me and Tom Thomas."

"And not me?" Lacey turned slowly and painfully forward and stared out the window at the thickening snowflakes.

"Take that up with Chief, Lacey."

A flashing red light whorled in the thickening snow and an ambulance pulled behind them. At the same time, two trooper cars pulled in front of them.

Three police officers left their vehicles and scrambled down the incline. Joey opened the car door, ushering in a blast of snow and cold air. "Stay in the car while a medic checks you over and I assist these officers."

"I'm coming with you; I believe that's Starr's truck." Lacey said.

Joey shook his head. "Nope. We'll find out who owns this Chevy Colorado. Starr has a GMC Sierra." He tapped her arm. "you better know your trucks if you're going to do this job."

His cell phone rang, and he answered, shifting to his other ear while the caller talked. Lacey watched his face for signs of the news, but she was unable to decipher anything.

Meanwhile, she turned her attention to an isolated spot on the road where two state troopers, a sheriff, and a medic were returning from the overturned truck. She could hear one of the policemen radio in for a search party to capture an elusive car basher. One officer left the group and drove off in the police car, its blue light spinning as it traveled expediently down the icy road.

When Joey got off the phone, he had a peculiar look on his face.

"Who was that?" Lacey asked.

"Chief Ringwood. They have transported your grandmother to the hospital. She was in an accident while we were dealing with your incident. Come on, we'll head over there as soon as the doc checks you over." He whistled between his teeth and waved. "Medic! Over here!"

With a few scrapes treated with bacitracin and Band-Aids, a splint on her left index finger, and a crutch for walking because of a sore ankle, Lacey was driven to the hospital in silence by a sheriff's deputy. Luckily, it wasn't a far drive. Lacey could only wonder how bad off Gran was and what had truly happened to her. If the car basher had been busy ramming Lacey, was it possible Gran had been the victim of another car basher? She did not want to jump to conclusions; however, the fact that Gran had been brought to the hospital was not a good sign.

The deputy dropped Lacey off at the doors of the emergency room, and she forged ahead agreeing to meet him inside the hospital.

The lady at the front desk saw her walk with difficulty through the entryway and asked, "Are you here to see someone or are you the emergency?"

"Likoudis." Lacey didn't have to finish with Gran's first name because she saw her mother walking into the hall while fiddling with her cell phone. Before Lacey could flag her mother down, her phone rang in her pocket, and she answered. "Look toward the front desk, Mom. I'm right here."

Lacey's mother started toward her, and Lacey closed the gap. Her head was pounding from the adrenaline rush from the car bashing incident. Her mom issued the warning, "Gran looks worse than she is. We have been trying to call you. Your father is furious that Gran went out in these conditions. Glad you're here, but, Lacey . . . where did you get those cuts and bruises . . . the splint on your hand . . . your leg?" Mom finally paused and waited for an answer.

Lacey relayed to her mother about her incident with the car basher. "Tell me about Gran." She could not hold together any longer and tears filled her eyes.

"Lacey, Gran only has surface wounds. She was lucky no organs were hurt when the airbag deployed. She got hit from behind and her car struck a pole. It could have been worse. She has asked for you since she was brought in; she claims she found the car basher and will fill us all in on the details when you see her. So, let's get in there and get this over with so she can rest."

Lacey noticed how tired her mother looked in that moment. Creases in her forehead aged her, and Lacey realized that her mother was getting worn down from worry. Now would not be the time to mention Vinnie Santora and how her job may be on the line, so she let it go.

Lacey and her mother walked into the darkened hospital room. Hunter O'Dunn sat in the chair by the window staring intensely at his hands. His jaw kept tensing, and Lacey could see that his face was flushed. A gasp escaped her lips as she took in the bloody mess of Gran's nose bridge and a huge gash across her eyebrow.

"Gran!" Lacey rushed to the older woman's bedside. "You should never have—"

"Oh, dear, don't be dramatic! When the airbag deployed, it smashed my glasses into my face and one of the lenses broke and took a bite out of my eyebrow. Trust me; it's not as bad as it looks." Gran gave a wan smile to Lacey to reassure her all was well. Lacey was not convinced.

"And what happened to you, Lacey?" Gran and Hunter O'Dunn asked in unison. Again, the car bashing incident was retold.

"Oh, Gran. No more investigating or rounding up the rosary brigade! You need to keep everyone off the roads on days like today and particularly during an active investigation! Please let the authorities sort this out. Now, tell me what happened."

Gran licked her swollen lips, and Lacey realized her face had taken the airbag square on. "Well, I was driving cautiously because of the condition of the roads and when I took a turn, a dark colored car appeared out of the blue and bumped me. I went into the pole and my car stopped. The airbag flew into my face, and I didn't see anything else. I feel certain it was the car basher because he hit me from behind and didn't stick around."

Lacey kissed Gran's forehead and twisted away suddenly. "I'm glad you're okay, but I have to go to the station. I want to talk to you later about the accident. You get some rest! The department may need information from you. I don't know what to tell you to expect, just be prepared to do some paperwork and an interview. I love you!"

Gran gave a tired smile. "I love you too, Lacey. Be careful out there."

Lacey was now in a hurry to talk to Chief. She was convinced there was more than one car basher. Her head pounded from the accident but more from considering the possibility that there could be multiple monsters targeting the elderly in their community.

CHAPTER 9

OUT OF ACTION

**Sometimes when things are falling apart,
they may actually be falling into place.**

Angel Chernoff, flickr.com

Chief Tadhg Ringwood walked toward the hospital as Lacey stepped outside the doors. "Hey, Lacey. Just the person I want to see."

Lacey tensed immediately, noticing Chief looked peeved. Thick snowflakes from a squall covered the two of them, and others bent over, hustling to find cover from the snowstorm. They dodged under the protection of the eaves of the hospital entrance and stamped their feet to knock snow off their boots.

Lacey found her voice, "I was just going to the station, Chief."

"Take the rest of the day off to heal, Lacey. Even a tough person like you needs a respite after an ordeal. You're banged up pretty bad from what I can see." He looked her over thoroughly and his voice became officious. "It's dangerous to give people like you information. I never thought you would pull a stunt like this." His expression softened when he calmed down several degrees and asked, "How's your grandmother?"

Lacey never cried. She felt tears welling in her eyes and willed the dam not to burst. She realized the day's stress was finally getting to her as she felt intense pressure on her forehead and behind her eyes.

"We're both fine," she lied.

"Don't act brave with me, Lacey. I know your grandmother will be fine because I've checked on her. Now that I see firsthand your cuts and bruises, I consider you to be one lucky lady. No, you are not *fine*." He cocked a thumb toward Parking Lot B and his official vehicle. "Let's talk in the car," he said, looking sideways at her and guided her by the elbow in a thoroughly annoying way. He wanted Lacey to fill him in, but he didn't want to hold up whatever was progressing at headquarters. "We need to be quick. There are developments at the jail. And I've just interrogated the person behind your grandmother's car bashing accident. Alex Karl will be staying in the hospital for a couple of days due to his injuries. He needs more questioning; he wouldn't reveal anything. Do you know him? Is he one of Santora's flunkies?"

Lacey nodded. "I don't know him well. I was gone when he joined Vinnie's squad."

"No need to worry about him going anywhere. He'll be out of commission for a while with a broken collar bone and a concussion but they're not serious enough to keep him out of jail," Chief said.

He took the lead strides toward where he had parked the car. He reached the passenger side first and opened the door as Lacey paused.

"Get inside where you'll be warm," he invited. "I'll turn the heat and wipers on." While he walked around to the driver's side, she just stared out the windshield at the snow that had not abated. Her brain was rattled by the whole day. She had started out knowing it would be a day to remember, but it was far past her expectations of adventure, and now Chief was taking command.

The cold blast from Chief opening his door brought her back to reality and she rushed to fill the silence. Finally finding her voice, and after telling of her episode with the car basher, she said, "What I don't understand Chief, is my grandmother and I were bumped from behind at almost the same time in different locations. While you and your team were clearing her wreck and arresting Alex Karl, Joey McGrath appeared at my crash scene minutes after it happened. He said you put him on the team." Her voice trailed off, not wanting to sound offended Joey was tagged to be there and not her.

"That's correct. I wanted to see how he would work with others. I feel he is ready for teamwork," Chief said, looking at her without flinching. "What are you thinking, Lacey?"

"We now know there are more than two bashers on the roads. My basher is still on the loose." She paused. "Were there any similar incidents called in?" Lacey held her breath. She didn't want that to be the case, but it seemed plausible.

"Not that I know of, and I was thinking the same thing. There are different colors on the cars that have been hit, meaning that we are up against a radical team of car basher cases."

Chief was used to being the one putting forth opinions for others to make judgments on, and while he had stressed that Lacey had overstepped her boundaries as a rookie more than once, he was relieved that Lacey had arrived at the same conclusion. He was simultaneously impressed. As a rookie, she showed a lot of promise, even if her decisions read as noncompliant. He would deal with her noncompliance the next day, he decided.

"Time has run out. I'm off to take care of business at the jail." He waved to a deputy parked in a spot ready to take over any official duty. "I'll have Deputy Johnson escort you home." Lacey exited Chief's car and awkwardly climbed into the deputy's vehicle. In a muddled haze and her body aching all over, she watched Chief Ringwood tear out of the parking lot with lights flashing.

Inside the jail, Chief Ringwood trooped into a large room tainted by a sour stench. A gang of thugs were lining up on a make-shift stage beneath harsh yellow lights.

"The road crew," a deputy announced to the chief after he had briefed the officers mulling about awaiting his arrival.

"Who are these people in the line-up?" Deputy Harris asked.

Chief said, "Blaze McCauley, and Maggie Longjohn are repeat offenders from Santora's squad. They are not necessarily car bashers. They could be drug dealers or ordered by Santora to do one of his countless dirty contracts."

Another officer rambled off the other names from a list in his hands. He conferred with Chief Ringwood who had a pile of clipboards he was perusing.

Chief stared at Blaze McCauley's black pupils that passed for eyes in his vacuous face. His eyes traveled back to Maggie Longjohn. Unable to focus, Maggie looked flaccid and helpless.

Missing from the line-up was Alex Karl. Alex remained in the hospital with injuries sustained while bashing Nadine Likoudis' car bumper. After sending Nadine over the embankment, injuring her and totaling her car, he flew over a nearby mound and landed his truck tilt-wise in a creek sustaining injuries to his shoulder and head.

Deputy Harris said, "I've known Alex Karl since Sixth Grade at Troy Central. He'd be the first one to give a hand." He swallowed hard. "How can you not know someone you've known for so long?"

Chief shrugged his shoulders. "People change—it happens all the time for reasons only they know."

"Anything else I should write down, Chief? I have all their names and personal info." Officer Harris poised his pen over his notepad.

Chief rattled off the information he had, realizing how inadequately he had investigated the wreck involving Lacey's car. He needed to question Rookie McGrath who had been on the scene. He had been so caught up in the commotion of all the wrecks that day that he had failed to ensure proper protocol. He sent a prayer that he would not regret his oversight.

"This finishes it, Jason," he said. "Fingerprint and book each of these perps, and then release them. The only one we can hold is Alex Karl and we can't do that until he's out of the hospital. Next, we need to find out who ran O'Dunn off the road. The perp who got away. He's out there somewhere."

Before Chief turned to leave the jail, he stared hard at the stage, envisioning Vinnie Santora standing there.

CHAPTER 10

MUTINY

Have Faith that everything will work out for the best.

Lacey limped into Chief Ringwood's office early next morning. She slept a full eight hours and still felt achy but rested. Even though his voice was harsh and projected a genuine Irish brogue when stressed, she intuitively recognized a strong magnetism developing between the two of them. She clairvoyantly realized Chief did not have a clue of the sensory feelings running through their veins.

Having had time to mull over the activity of the day before, Chief was not as tolerant of her actions as he was earlier. "Wipe that smirk off your face, O'Dunn. I don't have time for your dithering nonsense. Obstructing the law, that's what you did to this unit yesterday by taking the car bashing matter into your own hands."

"Oh m'god, Chief, those poor senior drivers. I had to try to help them. It's a wonder they didn't have heart attacks."

"One did," he reminded her.

She pressed her chest with bandaged hands, shock tingling through her. "I can't feel mine." Ever since she was rammed by the red truck and watched it sail over the edge and crash, her arrhythmia had been activated.

"That's an understatement." It dawned on Chief that he couldn't be sure if he was angrier that she had pulled this stunt or that she had ended up in a dangerous situation. He could not afford to end up going easy on her. He had to be fair to his other recruits, meaning he had no choice but to write her up and in time she could reenter the program. He told her so.

Lacey's decision to the reprimand she knew was forthcoming was the reason she had broken a pact she made with herself and taken a sleeping pill last night. To date she had been off all enabling medicine.

"I had to do this, Chief, especially when my mother told me my grandmother and her posse were canvassing the roads. I understand your position and I will take whatever discipline is coming to me." She added fervently, "After my penalty is done and I am clean again with the department, I plan to become a Private Investigator like my Uncle Tony Pastore. I cannot be restrained any longer with this program to become a police officer. I find it too restrictive."

A look of perplexity began to form on Chief's face. He stood up and took a few aimless steps around the room. He stopped behind her and put a steadying hand on her shoulder. "You have the Irish spunk and determination, Lacey. We need police officers like you. However, your actions have been too free spirited to remain with the force where you are expected to follow rules. I tend to agree with you . . ." He sighed. "A job in the private line of detecting may be more suitable to your nature."

Lacey tossed her head. "I've come to that conclusion, Chief. I consider being free spirited one of the perks of being self-employed. Joining the force is not in my future. I am sure of that now."

"Why am I not surprised." Chief dropped his large, well-toned frame in his battered leather desk chair. "And by the way, Tony Pastore is a first-rate detective. I work with him often. He'll be a good man to shadow."

"Uncle Tony has been my mentor since I was a kid with cowlick bangs. He recently solved the murder of Mavis Gordon, the wealthy entrepreneur owner of Willoughby Chase, a magnificent old estate in the Grafton Mountains."

Chief nodded his head and glanced at his watch before rising. The interview appeared to be over. "May I make a suggestion, Lacey?"

She nodded expectantly.

"Take a few days to heal and work through your admonition; finish this rookie program and you will blaze forward with the knowledge you acquire to be an exceptional P. I."

"Will I be able to work with the team on the car bashers in the meantime? I'd like to follow through with these crimes to the end."

"With restrictions. Remember, you're not a police officer in the line of duty."

Lacey pushed herself out of the chair with difficulty and shuffled toward the door. "Yes, Chief, I will finish the program and become a full-fledged officer. I agree the training will make me a more efficient P. I."

At that moment Chief Tadhg Ringwood became aware of the captivating Lacey O'Dunn. She was exceptionally beautiful, slender and graceful. Molly so often pointed out to him she could be a Vogue model. Was he so blind his manhood was just realizing this fact? Emotions stirred within him that he had not felt in a long time, and he refused to bring them to the surface. He moved away from the desk and opened the door in a gentlemanly fashion contemplating how *these revelations were going to complicate his life.*

And then Lacey flipped her silky blonde hair to one side as she habitually did and quipped, "After I hang my P. I. shingle and I have the privilege to work with you and your team on a case, you must play by my rules, Chief."

On the first day of administrative leave, Lacey felt well enough to do errands even though she felt stiff and achy all over from the recent accident.

The first stop was the Bennington Crafters Center early morning where Starr Ellis greeted her from behind a counter in the trendy emporium.

Lacey did not have it in her to play nice today. She was there to pick up the shawl she had ordered for her grandmother to give to Francis.

Starr said, "The only reason I'm here is to open for the owner because she's short-handed and I desperately need to make it to payday." She looked at the big clock on the wall. "Ten after nine. I want to scoot after my replacement arrives at 9:30. I begin training as a nail tech at a downtown salon today." She spread out her hands, showing off her manicured purple-tinted nails with pointy ends. "I can set my own hours and not clock in and out anymore. Say, how's your grandmother? I heard she was in an auto accident during that nasty snow storm last week."

"Improving," Lacey said cautiously. It dawned on her that Starr might not be aware that she, too, was involved in an accident on the same day even though her cuts and scrapes from some type of incident were obvious.

"Poor lady—must have been a fright for her," Starr said absently.

"Are you still seeing Vinnie?" Lacey was making small talk.

Starr tensed. "I told you before, I love the guy."

Lacey wondered if Starr thought she was convincing anyone that Santora was a good catch.

Lacey paid for and accepted her package. She said, "I see you don't have your truck back. Who did you say is doing the work?"

"My brother, Nelson. If you ever need a repair job on a vehicle, he's the best."

"I'll remember that, and I wish you well in your new career. I may need your nail services sometime. Stay in touch."

Late morning at the doctor's office, Lacey called Chief Ringwood to ask about the report from her cousin, Dom. Not wanting to get her cousin in trouble as she had before, she decided to call Chief directly to ask for results.

"Hi Chief, it's Lacey. Do you have new information about the latest accidents?" She adjusted the phone to her ear while she waited for the receptionist to call her name. The doctor had agreed to recommend a chiropractor for adjustments to her neck.

"Aren't you supposed to be resting?" Chief let out a sigh. It was apparent Lacey's idea of healing after her accident would consist of sleuthing from home. "There's nothing in the report other than a mention of additional paint colors. We've already discussed this." Chief huffed, knowing Lacey would check in with Dom later unless he answered her directly. He figured it was easier if he communicated better than he had in the past. At least he understood the language they were speaking now—solving a crime.

"What are the colors?" Lacey asked.

"Red and silver." Although she was a rookie and one of the lesser team members, he quickly filled her in on the arrests made and the citations given at the jail.

"I'm impressed. But it's hard to believe this many people would join up to bump elderly folks off the road in their cars for kicks. What color did you find on my grandmother's car?"

"Silver."

"Silver, and a red truck bumped my Subaru," Lacey added, her heart beating fast. "Tomorrow's forecast is snow, sleet and rain. That means it will be another black ice day."

"You're right on. It's the type of weather these maniacs thrive on to terrorize their victims. There'll be undercover on the back roads tomorrow. Hang by the phone and with luck, I'll be calling you." Chief knew Lacey wished to be back in the mix, but he was adamant she not be in harm's way again, especially while recuperating from one car bashing incident.

"I want to be there when you bring a car basher in, Chief, especially if it's Vinnie Santora. I would really like to tag along with one of your undercover officers."

"Don't even think of it, Lacey. I'll tell you where you can be helpful. We need to field some of the paperwork coming in today and tomorrow morning. We'll have to process all reports and arrests." Chief paused and then added, "Don't forget, you're still a rookie. I'm already allowing you to be involved more than I should."

Lacey knew the chief was right and putting her in her place was the professional thing to do. But she couldn't help noticing the undercurrent in his tone. One that sounded more caring than condescending.

CHAPTER 11

REVELATION

**Sometimes you need to let go
and see where the circumstances take you.**

The next morning, Lacey drove to the station early. Chief had beaten her there by an hour. She had noticed him pulling out of the parking lot at the apartment complex while she was rushing around getting ready. Ultimately, she was afraid he was sprinting to the station to pull a fast one by traveling with the undercover crew preparing to search the back roads for car bashers in the predicted snowstorm.

He looked up as she walked in. "Hey, ready to check the paperwork? We're definitely making progress." Chief looked angelic behind his desk.

As a peace offering, knowing her frustration the action would be elsewhere, Chief pulled four folders out of a pile on his desk. He tapped the top one. "This report is your grandmother's." He fanned the others. "I'm concluding that all of these vehicles have had similar accidents and the driver in each case has been over seventy, except your wreck, but you were disguised as an old lady, so the profile remains." He scratched his ear. "I'm convinced a truck was involved, due to the high point of contact with the various cars. It appears the bumper on the assault vehicle was covered with a cushiony wrap so it wouldn't leave evidence of an indentation or lose paint chips."

Lacey slid into a seat opposite Chief Ringwood. "I'm way ahead of you, Chief. I knew this when I was at my cousin Dom's body shop the first time it happened. And now I have experienced it firsthand." Lacey's eyes narrowed. "The only accident a car was involved was my grandmother's and that was Alex Karl's silver Toyota. And one of the suspects on the list of possible car bashers has been missing a truck the last couple of times I ran into her." Lacey was ready to share her hunch.

"Are you going to tell me?" Chief was growing impatient at the pause. He, like Lacey, was ready to get this over with, and he didn't like the thought that Lacey was withholding pertinent information.

Lacey recognized Chief's irritation and said straight away, "Starr Ellis claimed her red truck was being worked on the last two times I saw her. It's being repaired by her brother."

"Alright, let's drive together and go pay her a visit. Do you know where we can find her?"

"She's learning to do nails somewhere . . . I forget if she told me specifically, but there are only a few places to check that specialize in nails." Lacey shrugged. She knew it wouldn't be too hard to find Starr at one of the popular salons.

Chief cleared his throat. "I've known for some time that two of our rookies are buying drugs from Starr and her dealer, Santora. Sad to say, we've had all our rookies under surveillance and finally, we caught a break. A deal went down between Ms. Ellis and one of our undercover agents. With prison ahead of her, she cooperated with us and fed us all types of information." He tugged at his sleeve. "She admitted that she and rookie Greg Conners played 'bumper car' games for thrills. Vinnie heard them talking about it and made it a competition, which is how it got out of control."

Lacey turned her head to the side to look at Chief Ringwood. "Is there a reason you are just now telling me this information?"

Chief turned his gaze to Lacey. "You are still in training and have been recovering from being hit on an unauthorized undercover operation that could have gotten you killed." He pummeled the top of his desk with his fists. "We were still working the cases. I have victims and a family that will never see their loved one again. When I share things, it is out of respect, not duty, Lacey."

Lacey felt exasperated. She knew what he said was true, but these cases had landed in her lap, almost like providence—with Francis, Gran, and herself being targets, she felt invested. What Chief said was spot on, so she began devising her next plan.

CHAPTER 12

SHOWDOWN

Once is happenstance.
Twice is coincidence.
Three times is enemy action

Ian Fleming

Lacey knew that the perpetrators weren't locked up yet, much to her chagrin. When Chief left on an emergency call, she looked down at her nails and realized that she had an opportunity to gain some intel of her own.

Training was suspended on the weekends, unless a trainee wanted to use the police station gym, and with her administrative leave still in place, Lacey had time to pamper herself. She got in the car and searched for the salon she paired with Starr Ellis and its hours. "Opens at nine . . . Guess I have time for coffee before I get started." Lacey talked to herself in the rearview mirror as she put lip gloss on. Readjusting the mirror, she started formulating her game plan.

As she waited in the drive-thru for her coffee, she looked in her side mirror and recognized Vinnie Santora sitting behind her in line. He noticed her at the same time, locked eyes in the mirror, and grinned. Lacey felt her heart speed up.

At that moment for some reason she could not comprehend, she recalled her first meeting with his adoptive mother, a beautiful brunette, tall and graceful in stature. The most striking characteristic about Barbara Jillian Santora was her sad countenance, yet by appearances, she seemed to be a person who had it all.

Lacey vividly remembered staying one weekend in the joyless townhouse in New York City, richly embellished with artful décor and posh surroundings. There was an indoor pool, hot tub, and a vegetable and exotic rooftop orchid garden in a well-tended greenhouse overlooking Central Park. Lacey shivered at the memory. She had felt caged, trapped, and she'd been desperate to be anywhere but in the creepy, luxurious Santora townhouse with the draconian lord of the manor, Nicholas Santora, skulking about.

Lacey could vividly hear the undertones of concern for Vinnie in Barbara Santora's motherly plea; *Hopefully, you will be good for my son, Lacey. He needs a nice girl to keep him out of trouble. All the potential in the world, this one, but he seems to enjoy street games. For crying out loud, he could be the greatest mind of his generation if he could keep his hands, nose, and record clean.*

Lacey had been in no shape to make judgments back then, but as she waited for what seemed like eons for her medium black coffee, she recalled all the "minor" things Vinnie had pulled in their time together. He came across as charming if you didn't know him well and seemed to have the answers: *"It will turn out okay; don't fret; everyone does it."*

The things he said in private concerned her more. *'You will never get away from me. Don't even try. If you leave me, you will always have to look over your shoulder, and I will always be there.'*

Chills spread over her whole body. There he was.

The drive-thru window slid open, startling Lacey. The green-haired girl with bright pink eye shadow, too much eyeliner, and bright purple lipstick handed her coffee in a Styrofoam cup. "Have a goo'day. Sorry 'bout the wait."

"Thank you," Lacey spat back, sounding rude, as she pulled out as fast as she could manage, attempting to put distance between herself and Vinnie.

As soon as Lacey was back on the road, she seemed to hit every red light, and wished she was still home and snuggled into bed on this chilly morning. Fear laced her eyes as she decided to check her mirrors, and of course, Vinnie was in hot pursuit, flashing his lights, and signaling with his hands for her to pull into a parking lot.

Lacey slipped her hand in her purse, felt her Colt, and proceeded to pull into the nearest parking lot rather than have his high speed cause an accident to an innocent driver. Vinnie was pulling the passenger door open before she realized the doors were unlocked.

"What do you think you are doing?" Her outrage made him laugh.

"Oh, Lacey! What do you think *you're* doing? Joining the police force like you are better than the friends you left behind. Little Lacey gets clean and thinks she's better than everybody." His voice dripped and oozed with aggression.

"Vinnie, don't patronize me. I had goals and life plans, *LONG* before running into you." Lacey pulled her purse onto her lap. In such close quarters, a grab for her gun could prove dangerous.

"Look, leave us all alone. Stay out of it," Vinnie warned. "It's in your best interest to get the police off my tail. I will come for you if they get me; this is personal," he spat. Vinnie was blackmailing her! She couldn't believe it. Vindication stirred in her chest. She was surer than ever that she wanted to be the one to take Vinnie down—for all the crimes he had gotten away with and to prevent him from doing more damage in the future.

Lacey pulled from deep within and growled, "Get out of my car, Vinnie . . . NOW!"

Vinnie just sat there with a smug smile on his face. "Or what?"

"Get out of my car before I call the police department and report this meeting. I have an order of protection against you, and you aren't allowed to be around me. I'm not scared of you; you aren't intimidating me. I am no longer part of your world, and I will not protect you! Get out of my car." Lacey grabbed her phone and made a display of dialing 9-11.

Vinnie grabbed the door handle. "Lacey, I'll make sure you regret this . . ." He pushed the door open and exited her car, slamming the door with such incredible force that the car shook.

Lacey immediately hit the lock apparatus and focused on her breathing as she slipped the car into drive. She decided to hang back and let Vinnie speed off first, so she could be sure that he didn't follow her. With relief, she watched as he raced out of the parking lot.

Back to her original mission, Lacey continued to the salon she anticipated Starr would choose to work as a nail technician. Lacey was not one to spend money on luxuries like fake nails, but this was another covert mission to gain information.

When Lacey arrived at the salon, she saw that she was the first car at 9:07. *Great, I won't have to wait long.* Pulling the door open, Lacey said a quick, thankful prayer upon seeing Starr bent over a pop culture magazine, perusing news on the celebrities that mattered to the masses.

When the bells jingled as the door closed behind Lacey, Starr jumped up on autopilot. "The hairdresser is running late this morning. How can I help you?" When Starr recognized Lacey, she relaxed.

"I would like to get my nails done, actually. Is that possible?" Lacey liked that Starr's shoulders had gone down; it meant she wasn't threatened by her presence.

"Pick your color and come sit here." Starr motioned to a huge rack of nail polishes.

Still shaken by her encounter with Vinnie Santora, Lacey decided not to mention her recent meeting to Starr. She pulled a cool toned light pink and sat heavily into the comfy chair. "I don't want long nails, as close to natural as possible."

"I can do gel nails; they are more natural than the fake nails and more versatile for what you do. It will just look like a pretty paint job but will last longer." Starr was all business in her explanation; Lacey was impressed.

"That sounds great." Lacey nodded.

"The colors are different. You will need to pick from these." She handed Lacey a chart with different colors. All trendy, she decided on a shade close to her original choice while Starr pulled out a mini light to place Lacey's hands under as she completed layers.

Lacey and Starr fell into a comfortable rhythm where Starr would point toward her hand and Lacey would offer it as Starr began filing her nails. At first, the two made small talk, but Lacey gained her opening.

"Vinnie has been acting strange." Starr looked shocked that she had said it out loud to Lacey. "I'm sorry. I'm sure you don't care . . ." Her voice trailed off.

"Starr, it's okay. If you want to talk about it, we can. Vinnie Santora is in my past, and you don't have to worry about me." Lacey reassured. She was hopeful this conversation would lead somewhere productive.

"I didn't mean to bring it up, but it would be nice to talk to someone who might understand him." Starr seemed to wait for permission before adding more.

"You are safe talking to me," Lacey offered support without seeming too eager. She didn't want Starr to change her mind.

"Well, the last few weeks, Vinnie has changed toward me. We were having a lot of fun . . . on . . . er . . . a project, but when the conditions of the project changed, he acted like he ran out of use for me. Problem is, I thought he loved me. So, how can he just turn it off and ignore me unless he needs me? I know there's a good guy in there when he wants to be . . ." Starr kept pausing. This was clearly difficult for her.

Lacey squeezed her eyes shut. She knew all too well what Starr was saying. "That's Vinnie. It has nothing to do with you, Starr. Unfortunately, Vinnie has a lot of demons he fights with: the drugs, the alcohol, the criminal activity. It's hard to be close to people when you have a lot of guilt inside all the time."

Starr snorted. "There's not a speck of guilt in Vinnie." Then she let out a huge sigh. "Is there a way to free him?"

Lacey looked at Starr. "The only way that might work is if he deals with the consequences of his decisions. That has a way of reinforcing the rules and appreciation for life."

Lacey paused for a moment, and then said, "I'm sure you don't know the whole story about my association with Vinnie. He took advantage of the fact that I was young. I hung out with the wrong crowd. We would drink, but Vinnie got me hooked on drugs. I thought it was my choice to be with him, but now that I'm sober—it's clear to me, I would have never chosen a man like Vinnie. He is not kind or good. He says the right things sometimes, but he doesn't do the right things . . ." Lacey noticed the tears welling up in Starr's eyes.

"Lacey, do you think there's any chance he loves me?" Starr needed to believe she hadn't been used. No one wants to be a game to a human being they care about.

"Anything is possible. It is hard to imagine Vinnie loving anyone but himself, if I'm going to be honest." Lacey wanted to give her hope, but not of the false kind.

Starr stopped working on Lacey's nails to stare at her own. The inner battle she was waging played itself out across her face. "Lacey, I can't live with certain things on my conscience anymore. It makes me want to stay high, and I need to get clean, especially with a baby coming." Starr rubbed her tiny belly.

Lacey nodded. "I see . . . What do you want to do?" She reached over and pressed her hand to Starr's baby bump. "So precious."

"Will you help me with the police? I've already made a deal with Chief Ringwood but I haven't told him everything. I would like you to reinforce what I am going to say to him." She paused in her work and looked at Lacey with big sad eyes. "I know you can influence him. You two have a special bond, I've noticed."

Lacey wondered why everyone referred to a special bond between her and Chief Tadhg Ringwood. Were their feelings toward each other that obvious?

"I can't promise anything, but I know Chief, and his superiors have the ability to do what you are asking." Lacey didn't want to lose Starr's help at the last moment. "Can you tell me what is bothering you?"

"I'll start. We are almost done with your nails, and then I can take the rest of the day off because I'm in training." Starr started on the topcoat. "I am sorry to tell you that Greg Conners and I were together the first time we bumped a car. It was an honest to goodness accident, and we were terrified because we'd been drinking and he was in the rookie program to become a Troy policeman, so we took off. When we sobered up a bit, Greg seemed to think it was funny and he shot up with drugs. I guess I'm weak because I laughed along with him. Then he made a plan and even got a few others involved, and that's when it got ugly. Somebody died, Lacey; they died." Starr started to cry. Her face scrunched up and she could not hold back her tears.

Lacey stayed neutral, practicing her investigative interview style; this is how she would act when she was a Private Investigator. "Someone did die. What else happened?"

"I'd rather save the details for when they are recording the interview. I was only in the vehicle on the first bump. The media played their part. The more they focused on the wrecks, and especially when they started talking about 'car bashers,' well, that really set Vinnie and the guys off. They would read the newspaper and watch local news to get themselves recognized. It got gross to be around and Vinnie was using my truck to keep me quiet . . ."

Lacey watched as the drying light went off on the final topcoat. She told Starr, "You are talented with nails. Are you ready to go to the station? I can take you and we'll see what you need to do."

"I am very ready. I'll meet you outside after I let the boss know I'm leaving." Starr put things in the drawers they belonged in and gathered her jacket while Lacey paid the receptionist at the counter. Lacey headed out the door to wait in the car. This had gone better than she had expected, but it wasn't over yet. Not until the responsible parties were sitting in a jail cell waiting for trial.

CHAPTER 13

MISSING

Kidnapping causes a long-term rupture in the psyche of those kidnapped and of those who wait for their return. It doesn't end.

Uzodinma Iweala

Chief Tadhg Ringwood sat at his desk poring over the reports. They knew WHO, but they didn't have the motive or enough details to proceed with an arrest or prosecution. At this point, the prosecutor would call the cases hearsay and not press charges, and Chief needed to have something to offer the grieving family and other victims. Furthermore, he didn't want the type of people capable of this level of inhumanity to be free in his city to wreak havoc on other citizens.

Lacey came around the corner of Chief's office almost stepping on Foxy the Pothound. The small pointy eared dog stood up from his quilt-lined basket, growling, followed by a playful bark! Lacey raised her hands in a 'what's going on' gesture.

Chief explained, "I'm having painting done in my townhouse. The pup would be in the painter's way, and I didn't have time to place him elsewhere, so I brought him here."

Lacey noticed the canned dog food stacked in a corner. "Gran could take Foxy for a few days. She dog sits for her friends, among her other good deeds."

Chief's face brightened. "I may take her up on that. Will you make the arrangements?"

"As soon as I leave here." She dropped down impatiently into a chair. "Chief, we need to talk."

"Lacey, not now. You're still on leave for two more days, remember? Go pick out your Private Eye sign at the sign makers." He winked and leaned back against his chair as he shuffled a stack of papers on his knee. He was trying to focus, and her presence was distracting him from solving the cases he was determined to put to bed.

Lacey refused to be brushed off. "Whatever you are doing can take a backseat to what we need to talk about. It's urgent."

Chief couldn't hide his exasperation. "Your idea of urgent and mine might not match. Lacey, you have five minutes."

"I only need two." Lacy smiled with assumed confidence.

"Well, get to it. Your time has begun." Chief pulled her back to the moment.

"Starr Ellis is here. She wants to confess everything and will be able to point us to the evidence. She is asking for a plea deal in return for her account, and from my understanding, she is willing to be prosecution's *star* witness. See what I did there?" Chief groaned at the pun on the girl's name. "She told me of her meeting with you and a deal went down that day." Lacey flexed her long nails, wishing she could get used to their length. "She is ready to tell you more, Chief. Go easy on her."

"How did you pull this off, Lacey? Although, I'm not sure I want to know." Chief was watching her intently.

"See my beautiful nails? Starr has been feeling guilty about the victim that died, and it just happened naturally as I made an appointment with her at Victoria's Spa. I didn't do anything spectacular, just got my nails done." Lacey didn't mention that she had planned to dig for information. Surely, Chief would make his own inferences, and Lacey was fine with that. All that mattered now was the right people were about to be held responsible for their crimes.

Chief stood up. "You're done here for now. We will need to talk more about this later, and if this is worthy of a reprimand and another report in your file, I will be the one to put it there. You need to learn to stay out of things, even if the outcome is good. Oh, and I do appreciate your help with Foxy."

Lacey sat in the chair stunned. She had helped with the biggest case they were dealing with and wasn't getting red carpet treatment and congratulations. Instead, Chief was threatening another mark against the career she hadn't officially started. Inside, Lacey sank; doing the right thing wasn't always easy. She was trying to go up and above the call of duty, but instead she kept finding herself in the timeout corner. It was very confusing to her.

Feeling downtrodden after her meeting with the Chief, Lacey was about to leave the station when Molly called her name over the PA system. She went directly to the front desk and Molly greeted her.

"Good work, Lacey. You might still take some heat because you're technically in training. But you did well. Wait and see, Chief will come around." Molly had a generous smile.

"How did you know about my conversation with Chief?" Lacey was taken aback.

Looking cherubic, Molly gushed, "Will you look at that; the speaker monitor is turned on in Chief's office." She clicked it off and went back to her work.

Lacey shook her head at Molly and headed out into the cold.

Chief Ringwood finished the interview with Starr Ellis and sat in the chair after Starr had left, rubbing his temples. She had given him more than he expected. He sat musing about the abuse Vinnie Santora suffered as a child and smoldered at the thought of children like Vinnie enduring abuse of any kind at a trusted adult's hands. He dealt with these crimes too often. Still, it did not give a mature Vinnie Santora a license to become a wanted criminal.

Returning to the present, Chief knew where to find the car bashing vehicles and culprits. He knew what he needed to know about the drug ring that Vinnie Santora headed: where the drugs came from, who was dealing, who was using what. Chief was thankful for the breaks, but now he had to follow all the leads, create reports and investigation notes, and orders. He had to see about creating a task force, one he had requested, but the trustees hadn't wanted to spend extra funds on at the time, with so little seeming to happen in their city. Starr had just reinforced what he knew from experience: small cities weren't exempt from big city drug trafficking.

Chief felt a tinge of guilt. He had been tough on Lacey, and all she had wanted to do was help him solve the cases. She cared, and he had acted like her contributions to the station were a nuisance, instead of showing her the appreciation she deserved. He considered sending her flowers, but he knew his new plan to take her to dinner was more likely to make amends for his tone earlier.

He reached into his pocket and pulled out his cell phone. He tapped a number and let it ring. There was no answer, only an opportunity to leave a voicemail. He tapped again, still no answer. He vowed to try again later. Looking at the clock above his desk, he realized everything could wait until tomorrow. He would order flowers and take Lacey to dinner if she would agree with the arrangement. Both indulgences were long overdue.

After locking his office and leaving the precinct, he drove to the apartment complex but couldn't shake a dreadful feeling. Something was amiss. Lacey wouldn't leave his calls unanswered or unreturned unless something was wrong. Would she?

Her spot was empty at the apartment complex. A thin dusting of snow showed no tire prints, which made it clear she hadn't been there. Chief whipped a U-turn in the parking lot and made a hasty call to the precinct to obtain Lacey's parents' and grandmother's addresses. As he neared her grandmother's house he could see there was no car parked in the driveway and no new tracks. Gran Likoudis would be parked in the garage, so that wasn't alarming.

Chief could feel his intuition twisting his guts as he began to create scenarios of what may have happened to Lacey. Clearly, he cared about her more than he wanted to admit until this moment.

Chief didn't know where to look next, so he headed home. All he was sure of was that something didn't feel right. He made another U- turn and drove toward the back roads as dusk turned into a snowy night without the guided visibility of the moon and stars. It was a perfect night for car bashing unsuspecting victims.

CHAPTER 14

VENOMOUS

**Sweet are the uses of adversity which,
like the toad, ugly and venomous,
wears yet a precious jewel in his head**

William Shakespeare

Lacey came to in the dark. She had no idea where she was or how she had gotten there. The fog on her memory was lifting slowly; too slow. She could not locate herself, and it was not helping with her ability to figure this out. She decided to sit still and observe with the senses that were left in the pitch black.

A slow dripping sound gave away that she was underground. The echo and the chill as a furnace turned on told her she was probably in the basement of a house, but where? Her apartment didn't have a basement, and she remembered that she had not been home yet. She had left the police station and the temperature had dropped, leaving the slush on the road icy.

When Lacey went to move her hands to check her face, she panicked when she realized her hands were tied together. That was a bad sign; wherever she was, she was undoubtedly there against her will. The kneejerk reaction was to run, but her legs were tied as well. Inwardly she felt a growing dread. It was clear she was trapped, and her mind wondered if anyone was looking for her. Alarm set in as she realized that she was in a dangerous situation. The only way out, without a phone, was to get free of the rope, and it was tied well. She got to work immediately.

Chief let his mind wander while he slowed down on the curvy side roads. There wasn't a scenario that crossed his mind that was good.

The ringing phone jarred him out of his thoughts. Night dispatch rattled off, "Molly told us to call you, Chief. Lacey O'Dunn's car has been found at the bottom of a ditch on County Road 23. There is no one in the car. There are drag marks and footprints on the driver's side. Her car has the signature of the car basher cases. Please advise what you would like the officers to do."

"Start looking for clues to her whereabouts," Chief said as he fought against the rising panic in his voice. "I am on my way to the station. Have everybody there in ten minutes. I have some ideas, but I want to make sure we are all covering the bases until we find her." Chief clicked the phone off. He felt his heart sink drastically, knowing Lacey's car had been found without her in it. He said a quick prayer that she was well. His heart would never mend if the last words he spoke to her were a chastisement of a job well done. Would it have killed him to tell her good job? He would start appreciating his officers more, especially Lacey.

As he neared the precinct, he was clear on the search party plans. He was going after Vinnie Santora, and the other officers on duty could split up and check the other suspects and their homes.

The door at the top of narrow stairs popped open and a light switched on, causing Lacey to blink. She knew who it was before she saw him by the entry. Vinnie Santora clambered down the steps and was in her face in seconds. With her heart pummeling inside her chest, she squeezed her eyes shut.

"You're a real dumb ass sometimes, Lacey; I have your gun. Has it always been loose on the seat beside you in your car? That's scary. You should probably have some sort of lock on this thing." His mouth slurred the words and Lacey cringed. People on drugs or alcohol had no business handling a firearm. Vinnie, least of all. She prayed he would lose interest and put the gun down. Lacey remained silent as he rambled on. She desperately needed any diversion to occur.

"You squeezed my girl today. Now she won't take my calls. I couldn't find her, but I found you . . ." He slowly circled her, unsteady on his feet. "It was so easy, Lacey. You were driving down the road like you had not a care in the world." He sat down on an old sawhorse, stretching and crossing his long legs at the ankles in front of him. "Most likely your mind was on the Chief." He chuckled, looking relaxed as if he were playing a parlor game. "The rest is history . . . I intentionally bumped you off the road. Fast as quicksilver, I injected you with Midazolam in case you're interested." He coughed and spat phlegm on the cement floor. "Just a tad, mind you. Don't want you to have breathing problems on my watch." His thoughts trailed off and he abruptly quit speaking, leaving an eerie silence.

Lacey spoke just above a whisper. "That explains the headache, drowsiness, and nausea I'm feeling. Thanks a lot, Vinnie." She didn't want to scare or enrage him, but she wanted more information.

"I know you went to the salon today and Starr left with you," Vinnie accused. "I stopped in to see her this afternoon and her boss told me she took the rest of the day off. She left with a pretty blonde who paid with a credit card. I had her pull the slip, being concerned about Starr leaving with some strange woman, and what name do you suppose I found on the slip, Lacey?" His words slipped out rancorous.

"I got my nails done today, so what." Lacey would give him that much. She could prove that, plus he had seen the slip with her name and signature, so it wasn't like she needed to hide the fact.

"Where is Starr? I want to know RIGHT NOW!" He screamed so close to Lacey's face her ears rang.

"I don't know where she is!" Lacey was telling the truth, though it wouldn't help her.

"Where did you take her?" Again, his tone dripped venom, but his vituperative nature kicked her brain into overdrive. She had never seen him this violently angry before.

"We went to lunch and then baby shopping." She held her breath to see how that morsel of information had hit.

"Baby shopping?" He seemed too calm. "Who's pregnant?"

"I'll let you chew over that in your own time." Lacey felt herself fill with faux confidence in the situation.

"Lacey, I don't think you have this figured out yet. I am in big trouble for this one, and there's no way you're walking out of here this time. No freaking way, sweetheart. I saw you in the morning and you ran to get into my woman's ear. There is no way, after kidnapping you and holding you, I can let you go. You needed to stay out of it, just like I told you!" He was starting to ramble. Not a good sign.

"What are you going to do? Kill me?" She didn't have much to lose at this point. That's how he had made it sound.

"I don't know that I am personally going to kill you . . . I'm still figuring out what needs to happen. You are already missing . . . Maybe they'll discover you at the bottom of a lake? Pushed down a cliff by your buddy Joey McGrath?" He nodded maliciously.

Lacey's eyes widened and her heart sank as Vinnie described how Joey was one of his drug dealers. "Joey's car bashed *your* car on the night you and your precious grandmother got hit."

Lacey's subconscious knew it was Joey who struck her car as he slid into her passenger seat out of nowhere, conveniently coming to her aid. She did not want to believe it. Lesson 102 in her mental Book of Life . . . *Never trust.* She felt faint.

"I was an accessory to murder once," Vinnie sniggered, and went on as if it was an exceptional feat. "I never told you how my mother and I wasted my father, did I?" His pupils grew large, dark and cold as he pointed the gun at his heart. "My mother pulled the trigger while Daddy-O napped in his Lazy-Boy chair, and I watched. I was twelve years old. It was payback for the years he'd verbally and physically abused Mom, and sexually abused me, and my younger sister and brother. You didn't know that did you?" His cocky expression melted in a flash and in its place, she saw raw pain.

"That's right. My parents adopted us through a black market and that's when dear ole Dad's wicked streak came out. After mom pulled the trigger, the police wrote it up as a home invasion." His concentration suddenly switched to Lacey. "My life was ruined from the start. My birth mom didn't want me. My adopted dad got his jollies out of me and my siblings, and because of that, I turned to the only thing I knew I could trust. Drugs and dealing. You remember those days don't you, Lacey. How good it felt to escape the crappy world around you? I gave you that. You should thank me. So don't think for one minute I'm going to let you take me down. I am not getting locked up for this, so you gotta go!"

He moved to a chair and sat straddled backwards to watch over her. He pulled a syringe from his pocket. Lacey wanted to struggle free of the ropes, but proximity to Vinnie made that impossible, for the time being.

"I can't have you figuring out how to get out of this, Lacey. I need to be in control here. Me, not you." He lifted the syringe and flicked it with his finger.

With wide eyes, Lacey watched as Vinnie grabbed her arm, injecting her with whatever was inside the syringe. Struggling was futile. Had she been able to loosen the ropes around her hands she could have elbowed him in the throat and knocked the drug away.

The only thing Lacey could do was remain still. Vinnie was in control.

Even with a hazy head, Lacey's instincts snapped into focus. Fight or flight was kicking in. Her adrenaline pumped through her veins fighting against whatever Vinnie had given her. Lacey closed her eyes for a beat and swallowed hard. What she needed to do was prove to Vinnie he had her trust. That after all this time, she could still be his. It made her skin crawl, thinking that she needed to revert to the darkest time in her life—a time when Vinnie held all the cards and kept her compliant and hooked on all she had worked so hard to put behind her.

"Mmm," she muttered, leaning her head to the side. Lacey's eyelids fluttered but she wouldn't lift them. Not yet.

The chair in front of her squeaked on the floor, as if Vinnie had shifted it closer to her.

"I forgot how good this feels," she whispered.

Lacey braved opening her eyes. In front of her, Vinnie stared at her, his expression unreadable save for a glimmer of curiosity in his eyes.

"You miss it, don't you?" He leaned closer.

Lacey drew in a deep breath. "Mmm hmm." Hands still bound; she stretched her fingers as if reaching for him. Vinnie looked down and touched the tips of her fingers with his own. "I miss the feeling. The escape. Only you could give that to me, Vinnie."

Vinnie edged closer. She could feel his breath on her lips. The part Lacey was playing was dangerous, but it just might be the only way.

"You don't need Starr, Vinnie. You don't need a girl who's going to rat you out to the cops." The drug was beginning to take effect, but Lacey was prepared to make it even more believable. She slurred her words, "You don't need a baby to ruin things."

"I knew you missed me, Lacey. The drugs, the danger." Vinnie was close enough that they breathed the same air. "You've always understood me, but then you had to get cocky on me and prove you were above what we had."

"Not anymore," Lacey whispered. She let her eyes close, pretending she enjoyed the drug coursing through her veins. And when Vinnie pressed his lips to hers, she tried not to cringe, focusing solely on taking this as far as it needed to go to stay alive.

Chief Tadhg Ringwood pulled down the street where Vinnie Santora lived with Starr Ellis in her apartment in the city of Troy, not far from his precinct. He turned his lights off and adjusted his eyes to the darkness. He was going this alone so that everyone else could work in pairs, and if his hunch was right, he could get a few punches in that would end up hearsay from a criminal. This he was sure of; he did not want to add kidnapping Lacey to his long list of unsolved crimes.

Chief stayed in the shadows of the road in plain clothes. The only item giving him away was his CHIEF bulletproof vest partially hidden by his jacket. When he got one brownstone dwelling away, he pulled his gun out and made sure a bullet was chambered.

He drew near to the first-floor apartment door, and with the confidence only a warrant signed by a judge that understands the severity of a missing comrade can give, Chief kicked the door in so fast that had anyone been standing behind it, they would have needed medical care.

Once inside, he found no signs of anyone being there. He fully expected to find Santora and Lacey inside this building. Words tumbled over each other as he spoke into his lapel mike to his night dispatcher. "Sammy, find out which one of the perps we picked up knows where Vinnie Santora took his hostage. Offer him a deal and possible immunity. Pronto." He caught his breath. "Request permission for me to go inside the perp's apartment. Time is against us."

His heart palpitated when the mike buzzed a long minute later. "Alex Karl says Santora has a key to his apartment in a brownstone, same layout as Starr Ellis', two doors down from your present location. He gives you permission to go in."

"Makes sense; heading there now." Using the same tactics he used on Starr Ellis's door, he kicked in Karl's door, shattering it.

After hearing the loud crash above, Vinnie shoved to his feet and hurried to find a hiding place. The attempt at being a hardened criminal gave way to the scared little boy needing to cover an ego with the tough exterior. Lacey felt confident that the sound of a door blasting open was for her benefit and not Vinnie's. More than anything, she wanted to call up the stairs, *Down here . . . Please God, help, we're down here.* But she couldn't risk Vinnie learning she had been pretending. Like any good cop, Lacey couldn't blow her cover, even if help was imminent.

Faking a muscle twitch, Lacey jerked her leg, causing her chair to scratch across the floor. She couldn't see where Vinnie had scrambled off to, but she could only hope whoever was upstairs had heard her.

Chief immediately heard the sound and silently gauged where it had come from, much like playing hide and seek.

As cautious footsteps hit the stairs, Lacey felt the gratitude spilling over her eyes making a cold path down her face. She was both fearful and relieved to see Chief. But it was only for a matter of seconds before Vinnie managed to switch the light off on a nearby wall, sending the cellar into darkness.

Heart pounding, Lacey heard Vinnie scuffle behind her and whisper the most toxic words she had never imagined, "If you meant what you said, you'll stay quiet. Otherwise, I'll kill you both. Don't say a word without me telling you to."

Chief was immediately relieved to see Lacey was coherent and unharmed in his initial assessment before the lights went out. Swinging under the cover of a wide wooden beam, Chief attempted to gauge where Santora was hiding since the darkness presented little time to appraise the entire situation.

The barrel of the Colt pressed into Lacey's back as Vinnie hid behind discarded bedsprings to escape the view of Chief Ringwood. Lacey wasn't sure what type of a shot Vinnie was, so she opted to not call out.

Without saying a word, and hoping she was in Chief's line of vision as a dim yellow nightlight streamed from the open kitchen door above the stairs down into the recess of the cellar, she subtly shook her head cautioning him not to come forward. Chief picked up on the cue, since his eyes had adjusted to the dimness, and the light was glancing off her face from the doorway above.

Lacey and Chief made eye contact without Santora becoming suspicious, and she made the motion to where her tormentor was. She mouthed, *He has a gun.*

Chief nodded, pulled his gun from his holster, and with his heart thumping in his chest due to the close proximity of Lacy and Santora to each other, projected his deep voice from his position in the basement, "Vinnie Santora, come out with your hands up. This is your only warning."

There was a sudden moment when Lacey heard the striker behind her ready to discharge. In a quick action she lunged backwards into Vinnie causing him to lose control of the gun and it clanged to the floor. A twinge of pain slicing through Lacey's wrist made her gasp and a warmth pulsed down her arm. Somehow, her quick thinking had not only forced Vinnie to drop the gun, but Lacey had landed on an uncoiled bedspring, twisted just so to cut her arm. The blood gave her just enough slip to wriggle her hands free from the ropes.

In a swift move, Chief kicked Vinnie's arm as he reached for the gun. When he heard the smack of the weapon on the ground, he went full boar after Vinnie, wrestling him to the floor. Quickly, Lacey reached down and loosened the ropes around her ankles. She lunged forward, but stopped short to see the tables had turned, and Vinnie twisting around to straddle Chief, the gun poised and ready at Chief's forehead.

Her head still felt foggy, but the rush of the struggle had given Lacey the time she needed to pull through and find her bearings. Her brain switched into overdrive.

"Vinnie," she said calmly. "If you pull that trigger, if you kill him, you'll be put away forever. You'll be forced to say goodbye to me—to what we had and could have." The words felt like poison in her mouth, and she tried not to focus on the bewildered look on Chief's face. "I'm willing to go back to how things were between us, but you can't do this. You can't let them take you away from me."

It was just enough to allow Vinnie to tilt his head to look at her, and it miraculously gave Chief the upper hand. In seconds, Vinnie was on his back, then his stomach. Lacey's foot pressed hard against his spine as she grabbed the handcuffs Chief held out to her. She forced them around Vinnie's wrists clicking them tighter than necessary.

Instantly, Chief scrambled up from the floor and cradled Lacey's face between his palms. "Are you okay? Are you hurt? They found your car. I've been worried sick." Chief lowered his firearm into the holster and assessed Lacey's condition. He noticed her dilated pupils and a scowl immediately surfaced across his brows.

"What did he give you?" he demanded. "And please tell me you didn't mean what you said to him."

Lacey shook her head. "Midazolam. But I . . . I don't know what else." The wooziness was beginning to settle in causing her to feel faint.

Chief reached for her elbow and gently eased her down into a metal chair.

"And no, I didn't mean what I said to him. I was undercover." Lacey managed to look up into Chief's worried eyes and lifted her eyebrows.

"Are you sure this is the line of work you want to spend your life doing? You have been in two accidents and kidnapped in less than a month. These aren't good odds!"

Lacey caught her breath. "This was the worst by far. I think I'll be okay if you always have my back."

"What are you talking about Lacy?" Chief said humbly. "You had my back. You were in a life-or-death moment and you were the epitome of an officer who would never compromise her ethics." His voice thickened. "One of us could have been shot and killed. You are a hero, Lacy. You have earned a commendation with that action and I intend to present it to you." He gave her a bear hug. "There's one thing left to do, and he's all yours." Chief flashed a triumphant look.

CHAPTER 15

UNDER ARREST

"That's what arrest is: it's a blinding flash and a blow which shifts the present instantly into the past and the impossible into omnipotent actuality."

Aleksender Solzhenitsyn, The Gulag Archipelago 1918 - 1956

Ignoring the glare Vinnie shot at her, Lacey knew what to do and in a shaky voice began reading Vinnie his Miranda Rights as Chief yanked him off the floor: "You have the right to remain silent. Anything you say can and will be used against you in a court of law. You have a right to an attorney. If you cannot afford an attorney, one will be appointed for you."

Chief Ringwood addressed Lacey first, "Impressive." Then, he repeated the Miranda Rights to Vinnie so there would be no appeals based on who followed the protocol. In this event, he had doubled the necessary requirement.

As they stepped into the blustery, cold air, Vinnie couldn't help himself. He complained, "It isn't how it looks, Officer Ring-a-ding. Lacey and I go way back. She likes the scumbag life. Don't let her fool ya." He always had to blame someone else. Taking responsibility for himself had never been part of his character. For too long he had shifted blame, made others look guilty, and it had worked.

Chief Ringwood didn't even flinch or answer; he just led him down the street to the police cruiser. He stopped abruptly to hand his jacket over to Lacey. He had seen her shiver and decided that both Vinnie and he could tough it out in the cold to ensure that Lacey was warm.

He opened her door with his right hand, while holding a docile Vinnie with his left. He did not trust Santora and when he felt Vinnie slip, he let him tumble to the ground. The choice was to risk that they both fall or let the guy that took Lacey feel the cold hard pavement for a moment. He chose the latter and without remorse, drew his gun out of the holster on his waist to ward off any trick Santora may pull.

When he had situated a handcuffed Santora in the back seat and he made it around to his door to the driver's seat, he asked Lacey, "I asked this of you before and I know it's redundant but *are you okay?*"

"Other than drugs playing with my mind and my wrist," she held it out for Chief to see it was covered in blood, "I think I'm in shock but yes, I'm okay. I'd like to put this all behind me." Lacey was glad he was concerned, but she wanted to move past this part. To her surprise, she was struggling with emotions concerning Vinnie Santora.

"Well, for one, your car was found down a deep ravine, although the first report was ditch. You weren't in it, and this piece of garbage had kidnapped you. Where would you like me to begin being concerned?" Chief felt his frustration laced in his speech and he reached in the glove compartment of the car for a stack of napkins to apply to Lacey's wound. Why did this woman project independence all the time?

Vinnie chimed up from the backseat, "I love listening to y'all have a lover's spat, but when will I get my phone call? Can I make that now, so I can have bail money there by the time I'm booked in?"

"That's not how this works, and you know that from prior experience. No bail will be set for you, Mr. Santora, and it's a weekend. You'll see the judge Monday or Tuesday, and you can ask him about bail at that time." Chief Ringwood grinned as he took the wind out of Vinnie's sails.

When they arrived at the police station, Chief handed Vinnie over to the officers on duty. "Book him in and make sure he's got a secure cell. I will see you Monday; please try not to bother me until then."

After signing out Lacey's belongings an officer had gathered from her wrecked car, Chief walked Lacey to his official vehicle and opened her door again. "Before we do anything else, you need to be checked over by a medical team." He called ahead to get a doctor on standby for authorized police business.

After the doctor was satisfied Lacey had not sustained injuries needing immediate hospitalized care, he let her go and addressed Chief Ringwood. "The drugs should wear off with a good night's rest and plenty of fluids. I will send the report with documentation of abrasions and marks from being tied as evidence. The nurse obtained pictures that will help with the conviction. This young woman might need to see a psychiatrist to help keep her centered after the entire trauma. Other than that, she's fine."

"I will pass that recommendation along and see to it that she gets therapy for all she's been through. Although she's a quick thinker and saved my life. I'm the one who may need therapy. Thank you again, Doctor." Chief tipped his ball cap and sauntered toward Lacey, waiting to be driven home.

"I will accompany you to see your car at Dom's Garage Monday. For now, you should get some rest. And when we are off-duty, call me Tad." Chief looked at her surprised face.

"Ummm, okay?" Her visible confusion made him curl his lip up.

At the apartment complex, he walked Lacey to her apartment. He unlocked the door with her key she had dug out of her purse. Lacey was too exhausted to comment. All she wanted was a warm shower and her cozy bed. Although they would not take no for an answer, Lacy insisted she was fine and would see her mother, father and grandmother early the next day.

When they stepped inside her apartment a gas fire was lit in the fireplace. There was food and drink on the countertop. Someone had let themselves in to make sure her arrival home would be comfortable.

Lacey was speechless and unable to contain her emotions any longer. Against her will, she fell into Chief's arms and blathered like a baby. Several minutes went by before she pulled away from the comfort of a decent human being. Chief handed her tissues.

"Sorry," she choked. "I thought I was stronger than this. I've been through a lot more and never cried before, honest." She blew her nose. "Who did these acts of kindness, Chief . . . er, Tad?"

"I will attest to your Grandmother Likoudis and your mother. They were frantic with worry when they learned you were not at home and declared missing. Your father heard it over his short-wave radio. They called me to confirm the fact and insisted upon joining the search. I wasn't going to argue with two manic ladies, particularly your grandmother. I told Molly to immediately inform your family when you were located. The rest is history. And you made history m'lady. You are amazing Lacy."

Lacey dropped down on an ottoman next to the warm fire. She yawned and her immense weary eyes looked upwards. "I did what I had to do tonight, Chief . . . Tad. Sorry it's going to take time getting used to calling you Tad."

"I know it will take getting used to, but I want you to call me Tad. What you did tonight in that basement with a gun at your back was the bravest action I've seen in my time with the force. We both could have been killed. Remember, I am only a stone's throw away. Don't be afraid to ask for something specifically if you want it." He looked at her disconsolate spirit for a long time before he said,

"You are an amazing officer. Thank you for all you do. It seems I need you there and HERE. Meaning whether you choose to be one of my officers or a Private Detective, we can work together, either way. You went above and beyond duty tonight."

Lacey felt the cloud of darkness lift suddenly and she whispered,

"Thank you, Tad."

He pulled her gently to her feet, tilted her chin upwards, and kissed her fervently on the lips.

CHAPTER 16

TOGETHER WE ARE STRONG

Ecclesiastes #9

Chief Tadhg Ringwood answered the persistently ringing telephone before his front desk assistant, Molly, could snatch up the receiver. The phone was on his desk buried beneath a massive workload of paperwork. He was far behind with his job and now that the car bashing case was closed with a commendable wrap up by him and his team, he was anxious to solve a new crop of cases.

"Troy Police, Chief Ringwood here?"

"Chief Ringwood," Nadine Likoudis' distinct voice trilled. "Now I won't take no for an answer. I am inviting you this Sunday for an authentic Greek dinner with me and my family. Lacey will be there, and I want *you* to be a surprise *guest* for her."

Chief was speechless. "But . . . I'm Irish! I've never tasted Greek food." *Brainless thing to say,* he thought.

Nadia squealed with delight. "Come. One o'clock at my house on Sunday. 522 Floyd Avenue. And bring that cute dog, Foxy, with you. My family loves dogs. See you then, Chief Ringwood. And be on time, please." Click.

Lacey gazed fondly at her family and Tad Ringwood gathered around the dining room table at Gran Likoudis' quaint and charming two-story house with dormers and a white picket fence surrounding it. She watched her grandmother move agilely in a leg cast while setting a steaming dish of Mediterranean-style Greek clams on a placemat on the pine table.

In her mother's arms was Foxy, Tad's rescue Pothound, lapping up the attention he knew he deserved.

Nadine stood with hands folded looking cherubic and nodded to her son-in-law.

Hunter O'Dunn made the sign of the cross, lowered his head, and prayed, "Dear God, we have a lot to be thankful for . . . the safety and good health of Ma, Lacey, and Chief Ringwood and his good men in blue. Please keep our family safe this day and all days. Bless us O' Lord for these thy gifts which we are about to receive . . ."

"Amen," the gathered family and Tad Ringwood said reverently.

"I'm thankful for my Lacey, the cheek of her dressing as an old lady going after the bad guys." Gran wiggled into a chair beside her daughter, Nita, and kissed a squirming Foxy on his wet nose.

"She could have been killed," Tad Ringwood and Hunter said unanimously.

Lacey tasted baked eggplant wrapped in grape leaves. "This is delicious, Gran. A new recipe?" Her diversion tactic ignored the concern of the men, who should have learned that the two ladies sharing a moment wouldn't be easily convinced to stay out of the way when they had a mind to be part of something.

"Don't change the subject, Lacey," Hunter said irritably. "What you did was foolish and dangerous."

"Actually, brave," Tad conceded. "At first, I was angry, but now I have to admit it was a spectacular defense maneuver on Lacey's part, handling her car like a pro on an icy road and at the time not knowing who the renegade driver was, ultimately sending Joey McGrath's truck into the ditch." He hit her with his clear blue eyes. "Just don't do it again, please, *Miss Lacey.*"

Lacey stared into Tad's no-nonsense, deep blue eyes. She felt warm all over and blushed. "I'll do whatever it takes to protect myself and others in any situation." He turned away before the unspoken words were spoken. *And you, too, Chief Ringwood.*

"Couldn't you have left it to the police?" Nita asked, "Chief Ringwood and his squadron are capable men."

"Thanks, Mrs. O' Dunn. I'll pass your comment on to the men on the force. They don't get many compliments these days with pleas to defund the police signs all over the country. My partner and I weren't patrolling the road as planned for the reason we were attending to a three-car accident at the east end. By the time a team of my men reached Lacey, she had manipulated McGrath to drive his vehicle over a frost-heave, causing his truck to shimmy out of control and careen down a ditch. He had passed himself off to Lacy as one of the special team members. It wasn't until later we realized McGrath was the car basher." Tad shifted sideways in his seat and draped his arm over the back of Lacey's chair.

"When did you catch on to this string of hoodlums?" Hunter asked with his mouth full of crusty bread spread with warm, oozing butter.

"The arrest came together as a result of forensic evidence gathered at the crime scenes, in addition to following several leads with the cooperation of other area police agencies. We knew from past incidents we were dealing with a dangerous gang headed by Vinnie Santora." All together the family looked at one another, edgily recalling their battle with this evil one, who at one time controlled their daughter and granddaughter.

Tad continued, "Drugs and thrills were a factor. It turned out that Starr Ellis, along with several of her drug addict boyfriends, including Cahill and McGrath, in the rookie program with Lacey, came up with the idea to play risky winter road games. When McGrath admitted to bumping Lacey's car off the road, he turned informer to save his skin." He put his arm around Lacey's shoulders and gave her a gentle squeeze. "When Santora kidnapped Lacey, we had him. Fortunately, we have a good ending."

Everyone's face froze, including Lacey's when Tad added soberly, "That's not always the case." He pressed his lips together. "It was a close call as we all know, one I'll notch on my gun belt, thanks to Lacey." He rubbed her arm softly. "We'll be putting these lunatics behind bars for a long time."

Tad pushed away from the table and patted his stomach, "Excellent meal, Mrs. Likoudis."

Gran looked contentedly from Tad Ringwood to her granddaughter. She placed her dimpled hand over her heart and said, "A big thank you from my Rosary group, Chief Ringwood, and please join us again soon for a family meal."

Then she leaned across Nita and nudged Lacey. "When your grandfather and I started dating..."

Lacey put down her silverware. "Gran, where are you going with this? Are you inserting yourself in official business?"

"I'm just saying, I called this fated attraction when I first saw Chief Ringwood at the apartment complex. Remember . . . hubba hubba!" Gran looked mischievously at Lacey and Tad. *Wink . . . wink.*